whispering hills murder

Travel Writer Mystery Series - 4

wendy meadows

Majestic Owl Publishing LLC
P.O. Box 997
Newport, NH 03773

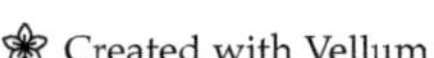 Created with Vellum

chapter one

"A what?" Patricia McKay asked as she munched on an apple while standing outside of an old barn with her cell phone tucked into one ear. A light snow was falling, and Patricia was eager to get back inside her warm farmhouse and find a hot cup of coffee.

"A Dead and Breakfast," Edna, Patricia's boss, repeated in a determined voice. "It's a…well, think of the board game Clue."

"Clue?" Patricia asked, feeling frozen snowflakes landing on the tip of her nose. The snow brought back memories of a dangerous mystery she had survived while being stranded in a snow-covered desert in Arizona. "Edna, I came outside to feed my milk cow, not talk about some silly…whatever it is."

Edna rolled her eyes. Inside her mind she saw Patricia dressed in clumsy farm clothes and holding a pitchfork. Patricia was actually dressed in a heavy green winter coat covering a brown dress, but to Edna the fashion statement matched hillbilly farm clothes. "You're becoming dull," she complained, walking back to her cluttered desk and plopping down on the edge.

"What? I'm not *dull*," Patricia insisted.

"Patricia, I'm wearing a very stylish gray dress. What are you wearing?" Edna asked.

"Well...." Patricia lowered a pair of beautiful eyes down to the green coat she was wearing and gulped. "I...my old coat and a brown dress—"

"And I bet your autumn-colored hair...hair that is so beautiful, by the way...is just dangling loose in the wind, right?"

Patricia raised her left hand and touched her hair. "I... well, yes." She gulped again and then quickly focused on the old milk bucket whose handle was stashed in her right hand. "Look, I have a cow to milk."

"No, you have an assignment," Edna corrected. "I want you to drive to Ohio and spend a week in the Dead and Breakfast."

"Drive?" Patricia asked as a gust of icy wind blasted her beautiful face. Patricia threw her eyes up at a dark, cold sky and watched the snow fall. "Why can't I fly?"

"Because the airlines and I are having a squabble right now," Edna snapped. "The company account was overcharged by five thousand dollars and until I get a refund my travel writers are state-bound and road-bound."

Patricia winced. "Edna, I was due to travel to Europe in two weeks—"

"Change of plan," Edna confirmed in a stern tone. "You're going to spend a week in Ohio and then write about a new bed-and-breakfast we're going to put on the map." Edna hurried behind her desk and sat down in a black desk chair. "Look, kiddo, I'm the world's biggest mystery fan. I love the game Clue...the movie, not so much. When a friend of mine told me about this bed-and-breakfast, I knew a gold nugget had been dropped in my lap."

Patricia sighed. Edna was a kooky boss who sometimes veered off the road to see the world's largest ball of yawn. It appeared, Patricia thought, that Edna was about to send one of her—not to brag—finest travel writers to write about a dorky attraction that no one would ever care about. But Edna was the boss and the boss issued the paychecks. "So much for seeing Poland," she sighed.

"Forget Poland," Edna insisted. "You're going to Ohio. Now go pack. I want you on the road first thing tomorrow. You're due to check in on Thursday."

"But…that's two days away."

"You better make tracks, then," Edna demanded and then dropped details into the air. "You are to drive to Whispering Hills, Ohio, and check into the Dead and Breakfast on Shadow Lane—"

"How appropriate—"

"Hush," Edna snapped and then rolled her eyes again. "If I didn't love you more than my own daughter, I would fire you."

"You'll never fire me," Patricia sighed. "And you'll never divorce your husband no matter how much you complain about him, and you will never disown your daughter for becoming a 'therapy clown,' as you say, instead of a 'real' doctor."

Edna made a sour face and then shrugged her shoulders. "You're right," she said and then continued. "You'll spend six days and seven nights at the bed-and-breakfast."

"And?" Patricia pressed.

"Well—" Edna paused and then nibbled on her lip. "I… kinda promised the owners you would help them create a murder mystery…write out a script for them while you're there."

"You promised them *what*?" Patricia dropped the milk bucket she was holding. "Edna—"

"Come on, kiddo, it'll be fun. You're a great mystery writer, and you've solved some hair-raising murders. Besides, you'll have six whole days to write out the murder mystery—"

"In exchange for free lodging, I'm sure," Patricia stated in a sarcastic tone.

"Well…." Edna winced and then eased forward. "A penny saved is a penny earned."

Patricia moaned. "Edna…I…."

"Have bills to pay, right?" Edna answered in a voice that pushed Patricia into a tight corner. She added in a motherly voice: "I sign the paychecks, remember?"

"Thanks for twisting my arm," Patricia fussed and then simply lowered her head. "Okay…Okay, Edna, you win," she caved, speaking as if someone were attaching her to a torture device. "I'll go to this so-called Dead and Breakfast and write out a silly murder game plot for you…but I want a bonus."

"You'll get paid your regular pennies. No bonuses will be issued until the airline refunds my money!" Edna declared and then hit her desk with a hard fist. "No one cheats Edna out of her pennies, kiddo."

"Yeah, tell me about it." Patricia rolled her eyes. Edna was cheaper than Ebenezer Scrooge refusing to pay a few extra pennies for a piece of bread.

"Watch it," Edna warned.

Patricia winced. "What's the address, boss?"

"That's more like it." Edna grinned. "Put 181 Shadow Lane into your GPS. Remember the town?"

"Whispering Hills."

"Good girl," Edna said. "Whispering Hills is in northern Ohio next to Lake Erie, so dress warm…but not like some backwoods hillbilly."

Patricia felt a cold chill run down her spine. It was the middle of January and Edna was sending her to northern Ohio to a frozen town scarred by torturous winter winds that roamed Lake Erie. "I'll dress warm," she promised. "I guess I better go milk my cow and then make the needed preparations…and I guess I better call Brian. We had a date set for tomorrow."

"What do you see in that guy?" Edna complained, not for the first time. "Every guy in the world would cut off their right leg just to get your phone number, and you're settling for a hillbilly cop."

A grin touched the corner of Patricia's mouth. Brian wasn't a hillbilly cop, but she always found Edna's exaggerations amusing. "Look, Brian is a good man, and we're to the point in our relationship where he finally accepts my career. Things are…good between us…and I'm happy."

"Good grief," Edna said, "you are a strange one."

"Am I?" Patricia asked as her mind suddenly ran to Ireland. Her last assignment had ended with her being caught in a strange mystery that didn't exactly end; the case was left practically unsolved. But at least no one was killed and Patricia was glad for that. "I guess I might be strange. Maybe that's why Brian likes me."

Edna bit down on her tongue. She didn't have the time or the energy to fuss about Brian Johnson. "Look, kiddo, let's get back to business," she demanded. "Your job is to write a great murder mystery for Mr. and Mrs. Benjamin Graves—"

"Graves?"

"Yes, Graves," Edna popped. "I agree, the name fits the Dead and Breakfast."

Patricia pulled her coat closer as falling snow grew stronger. "Okay…so I write the mystery—"

"And then write a great piece about the Dead and Breakfast," Edna instructed. "I want to put this place on the map."

"But, Edna…I write humor pieces, remember? Why me? Why not send Heather?"

"Because Heather couldn't write a mystery if she sat down on a toilet with a hand floating in it with the killer's name attached to it."

"That's…gross, Edna," Patricia stated in a disgusted voice. "No visuals, okay?"

"You're a great humor writer," Edna explained, "and you're also a great mystery writer. You're going to write a fun bed-and-breakfast mystery. So use your skills in humor and mystery to write a piece of work that will attract people from all over the globe." Edna drew in a deep breath. "Look, I'm a huge mystery fan. I love mysteries…. I play the game Clue as often as I can with my husband…even though he cheats, the rat. Why, I eat, sleep, and dream of the game Clue—"

"Exaggerating, aren't we?'

Edna wrinkled her nose. "Look—"

"Just tell me the real reason you're so keen on this. I know you love strange attractions, but my gut is telling me you have a hidden agenda," Patricia spoke in a careful tone. "Come on, spill the beans."

Edna hated it when Patricia spotted the cards she had hidden up her sleeve. "I'm going to fire you one day."

"No, you're not," Patricia replied. "Just tell me, what's the game…besides Clue?"

"Okay…all right…." Edna bit down on her lip with angry teeth. "There's a new attraction opening up in Oregon…a chain of bed-and-breakfast themes—"

"Mystery themes, I'm assuming, right?"

"Well…yes—"

"And Joan Tralles got to the golden nugget first?" Patricia asked.

Joan Tralles was Edna's business enemy, a woman Edna was always at war with. Joan owned her own travel magazine and was always trying to destroy Edna.

"And I'm guessing the gold nuggets you claimed fell into your lap required a little digging, right?"

"So, I called an old friend and asked a few questions—"

"You called Pete in research and told him to find you the closest mystery bed-and-breakfast," Patricia corrected.

"You're fired."

"I'll go write for Joan," Patricia threatened.

"You're rehired. Go pack and be on the road first thing tomorrow."

Patricia grinned. "Okay, boss, I'll accept the assignment and help you fight Joan," she promised. "I've never liked Joan Tralles that much myself. She's a bit of a snot."

"You bet she is," Edna claimed and then hit her desk again. "Joan stole Oregon away from me, but we're going to turn Ohio into a gold nugget! Now…go pack. I have to call the airline and threaten them with a lawsuit."

"Go get 'em, Edna," Patricia laughed and then ended the call and hurried to call Brian. Brian answered on the first ring. "Brian—"

"Our date is off because you're going on assignment, right?" Brian asked, sitting in his warm office reading over a case file.

Patricia felt her heart break. "I'm going to Whispering Hills, Ohio, for a week to write about a place called Dead and Breakfast."

"What?" Brian said. He lowered the case file in his hand and made a strange face. "Is this a joke? It's the middle of winter, Patricia. Why would Edna send you to Ohio? Ohio is snowed in—"

"I know, I know," Patricia said and then quickly explained the reason for Edna's impulsive assignment. Brian listened and then shook his head as she continued. "I have bills to pay —and hey, at least I'm staying in the country, right? And…I was thinking…maybe you could accompany me? Might be fun. We could take my new spruced up motor home."

Brian thought about Patricia's 1978 Winnebago and then smiled. "I guess I did go overboard," he confessed. "But that's behind us."

Patricia reached down, picked up the milk bucket she'd dropped, and hurried into the barn. "Yes, it is," she promised, walking toward a wooden stall housing a sleepy milk cow named Betsy. "So, you'll go with me?"

"I can't, Patricia. Wish I could," Brian stated in a miserable voice as his smile faded. "The state is breathing down the department's neck about an old case that took place last year. Seems like someone dropped the ball down in Atlanta and wants to pin the blame on us. But I'm not going to let that happen."

Patricia paused outside the wooden stall and glanced around the shadowy barn as the smell of cold hay filled her nose. "I...understand. Work is work," she said in a disappointed voice and then quickly added, "Your work is far more important than mine."

"Not true."

"Yes, it is," Patricia insisted. "Brian, you're a cop; I'm a travel writer. Do the math and you'll see the true answer. But hey, I'm not putting my job down. I love my work, but I understand that protecting our community from a bunch of bureaucrats is far more important than spending a week at some silly bed-and-breakfast."

Brian picked up his mug of coffee and took a sip. He respected Patricia for respecting his job. "I'm sure you'll have a good time, Patricia. And it's like you said, you're not leaving the country, so it's not like you're really leaving me. And who knows, if I get this mess cleared up in time, I might be able to drive up and join you."

"Maybe," Patricia stated but didn't get her hopes up. "I'll miss you. I was really looking forward to our date tomorrow night."

"I was too," Brian replied as Patricia's beautiful face consumed his mind. Oh, how he loved that woman...deeply. "When you get home, we'll pick up where we left off, okay?"

"Promise?"

"I promise," Brian said with a smile.

Patricia felt a gentle smile touch her heart. *I guess someday Brian and I might end up husband and wife,* she thought, then said out loud, "Well, I came out to the barn to get some milk from Betsy…uh…can you feed her while I'm away?"

"Don't I always feed all of your animals while you're away?" Brian teased.

Patricia blushed a little. "I guess you do…and without getting paid too," she tried to joke. "I guess Old Betsy can pay you with her milk?"

"Old Betsy would kill me if I tried to milk her," Brian laughed. "I can feed that cranky old cow but that's as far as I go and—" Brian heard someone knock on his office door. "Hey, the chief is here. I have to go. I'll call you tonight, okay?"

"You better." Patricia sadly ended the call. She looked into the stall and spotted the milk cow chewing on some old hay. "Well, girl, it's freezing cold, I'm about to go to some lame bed-and-breakfast, my boyfriend is busy with his work, my boss is insane—and you're chewing on hay. I'd say the situation is pretty normal considering it's my life." Old Betsy raised her head, looked at Patricia, and simply swished her tail a few times. "I guess that means I can get some milk, huh, girl?" Patricia sighed and then went to work as her mind settled down onto her new assignment. "Dead and Breakfast…good grief."

"It's freezing," Patricia mumbled under her breath as she swung her SUV into a snow-covered parking lot and bravely dashed into a Denny's that appeared to be deserted. A chubby waitress, who looked to be no older than sixteen, glanced up from a sleepy counter, lowered a strange-looking cell phone, and forced a weak smile onto a face polluted with bitterness and hate.

"I'm a little lost. My GPS stopped working on me,"

Patricia stated as she began shaking snow off her pretty pink coat. "I'm trying to find Whispering Hills."

The waitress stared at Patricia with sour eyes. Patricia was beautiful and slender—the type of woman the waitress despised. "Whispering Hills is the next town over," she told Patricia in a cold tone, hoping to get rid of the woman. "Just stay on Highway 16 for about another mile and turn onto Route 5."

Patricia nodded. "I thought I was close," she said and then studied the deserted Denny's. "It's getting late. I think I'll order a coffee and a cheeseburger for the road along with a side of fries."

The waitress fought the urge to roll her eyes. "It'll be a few minutes," she told Patricia and then wandered away to a sleepy kitchen, leaving Patricia alone.

"Nice girl," Patricia whispered. "Looks very happy." Resisting the urge to allow her mind to offer any clearer observations attached to human nature, Patricia glanced around the Denny's and sighed. "This area is under a blizzard watch and here is yours truly standing in this dive…far from home…preparing to eat a greasy burger and down some coffee that was probably made yesterday. Yeah, life is grand."

Movement caught Patricia's eye. She spotted an old couple stand up from a booth. Patricia, having assumed the Denny's was devoid of customers, was shocked to see the old couple begin walking toward the front counter. She quickly put on a pleasant face and offered a warm wave. An old man waved back and then began donning a thick gray coat. "I see you've been trapped into eating at this horrible place as well."

"Horrible indeed," an old woman said with a frown as she slipped on a heavy blue coat. "I may end up in my grave sooner rather than later."

"Now, dear," the old man pleaded with his wife, "let's not talk that way."

The old woman shook her head. "I'm seventy-two years old and you're seventy-four. We're not young chickens, you know." The old woman motioned around with a wrinkled hand. "We stopped to get a simple cup of coffee and to rest our old bones a little before driving on. We made the horrible mistake of ordering a simple hamburger plate. First the meat was undercooked and then the meat was burned. If you want my advice…run."

"Well, I admit we had to send back our order a few times, and the chubby waitress wasn't very pleasant. But Jesus teaches us to be patient and loving, dear," the old man reminded his wife and then smiled at Patricia. "Where are you heading to, young lady?"

"Oh…I'm driving to Whispering Hills," Patricia explained and then quickly called out. "Cancel the cheeseburger and fries…and the coffee."

"Smart girl," the old woman told Patricia and then asked: "Why on earth are you driving to Whispering Hills?"

"Awful place," the old man stated and then shook his head as if someone was pinching his arm. "Horrible people… sour town…sour land. The whole place is no good. Me and the wife make it a point to drive around Whispering Hills when we drive to visit our grandchildren."

"I…the photos I saw online look…pleasant," Patricia struggled to claim. She was exhausted from a very long drive with very few stops in between. Now she was being told that Whispering Hills, the town she was doomed to be trapped in for six days and seven nights, was…sour.

"Photos are deceiving," the old man warned Patricia. "Whispering Hills is a cursed town…cursed from the inside out."

"Cursed?" Patricia asked. "I don't understand. The research I conducted on the town—quick research, I'm afraid —didn't result in anything horrible. Whispering Hills appeared to be, at least to me, just another small Ohio town."

The old lady spoke up before her husband could. "The town is cursed, young lady. Stay far away."

"People have died there," the old man added in a low, creepy voice. "I grew up in Whispering Hills until I was sixteen, when my parents finally got enough smarts to move away. I know what goes on in that town. I know the secrets...I saw people vanish."

Patricia felt a silent moan leave her heart. "I'm a travel writer. I'm afraid I'm on assignment," she confessed and then checked her coat. "I'm due at a bed-and-breakfast, and I'm already running late. I was supposed to arrive at noon but my GPS stopped working. Looks like I don't have a choice in the matter."

"Turn around and go back home," the old lady warned Patricia and then reached out and grabbed the younger woman's gloved hands. "My husband is right...people die in that awful town." With those words the old man reached into his coat pocket, pulled out a twenty-dollar bill, tossed the money down onto the front counter, and then grabbed his wife's hand. "Whispering Hills is a cursed place," the old lady said.

"Cursed." The old man nodded and then hurried his wife out into the snowstorm.

Patricia walked to the front glass door, watched the old man help his wife into a gray SUV, and didn't move until the SUV vanished into the storm. "Cursed. Great, just great," she said and then pushed her way out into the snow just as the waitress stationed herself back behind the front counter wearing a hateful expression. Patricia tucked her head down against the cruel wind, fought her way back to her tired SUV, and crawled into the driver's seat. "Time to call Edna," she said and hurried to fish out her cell phone from her cold green purse.

"Where are you?" Edna snapped, picking up on the first ring.

Patricia didn't answer at first. Instead, she watched the heavy snow beginning to turn into a thick white blanket on the front windshield. "My GPS stopped working on me. I got lost, but I'm back on track. I should be in Whispering Hills within the next hour."

Edna picked up a blue pen and began tapping it against her desk. "I'm a lady who works long hours, kiddo, but let me tell you, waiting for you to call is worse than working a sixteen-hour day. You really had me worried. Why in the world didn't you answer my calls?"

"My cell phone lost reception until about half an hour ago. The area I'm in is under a blizzard watch," Patricia explained as she watched the front windshield turn white with snow. "Edna, look…I just ran into two people who claim Whispering Hills is a cursed town—and I'm apt to believe them. Nothing has gone right for me so far on this trip. First, I had a flat, and then the oil light on my SUV came on, and then my GPS stopped working. On top of that, my hotel reservation last night was misplaced and I was forced to hunker down in a hotel that wasn't exactly…kosher. I'm tired, hungry, and I just want to turn around and drive home."

"Nothing doing," Edna snapped. "You're almost to Whispering Hills. You might as well stick with it!" Edna threw down her pen. "Patricia, we're not going to let Joan win; do you hear me? Now, I admit that Joan has the high ground right now, but I have faith that you're going to turn a lame bed-and-breakfast into a real hit! We're fighting for the underdog!"

"You're a nut," Patricia told Edna in a tired voice. "I love you like a mother, but you're a nut—and I must be a nut for agreeing to take this insane assignment." Patricia shook her head. "I better get on the road before the storm shuts me down for good. I'll call you when I arrive at the B and B."

"That's my girl," Edna said and then quickly added, "Just a side note. I did some checking and there have been a few murders in Whispering Hills in the past. More than you'd expect for a town that size."

"What?" Patricia gasped. "Edna—"

"Just more flavor to add to your article," Edna insisted. "You know the old saying: 'Take a lemon and make—'"

"Bleach!" Patricia snapped and then leaned forward and began banging her head on the steering wheel. "Why do I work for her...why?"

"I heard that!"

"Yeah, I guess you did." Patricia grimaced and raised her head. "I just keep reminding myself I have bills to pay."

Edna grinned. She loved Patricia's spunk. No other travel writer working under her command had the nerve to back talk her, but Patricia...Patricia was special, not to mention brilliant. "Get on the road or you're fired."

"I'll happily accept being fired and stand in the unemployment line," Patricia assured Edna and then sighed. "Then again, I have my animals to feed."

"Call me when you arrive," Edna said, grinning as she ended the call.

Patricia put her cell phone away, hit the wipers, waited for the windshield to clear, and then cautiously got her SUV moving. "Cursed town, murders, Dead and Breakfast—I can't imagine what kind of nightmare I'm about to walk into."

Resisting the urge to drive back to Georgia, Patricia aimed her SUV toward Whispering Hills, clicked on the radio, and carefully drove through a raging snowstorm that showed no signs of letting up.

"*The storm front is expected to become worse overnight. People are advised to stay off the roads and stay in their homes,*" a concerned-sounding news reporter spoke into the SUV. "*Wind gusts are expected to reach eighty miles per hour. Up to three feet of snow is expected to fall before morning. The wind chill is expected to drop below minus ten degrees. Folks, we're in for a whopper of a storm.*"

"Great," Patricia said in a nervous voice as she fought her way through the storm, barely managing to stay on the snow-covered roads. For a short while, Patricia actually believed the winds were going to throw her SUV off the road and trap her in a deep snowdrift. But somehow—by grace alone—the SUV managed to stay on the road without being turned into a frozen, twisted heap of metal that some tow truck driver would have to haul away. "Easy now…just stay on the road… focus on the road," Patricia whispered as the last of the daylight was swallowed up by a vicious night. "Just focus on the road."

Over an hour later, after nearly missing the turnoff for Whispering Hills, Patricia drove through a dark, cursed town that held a low growl underneath its murderous closed eyes.

"Now…where is 181 Shadow Lane?" she asked, slowly driving down a deserted main street that didn't have a single lamppost offering light to the frozen sidewalks and closed stores hugging the street. "Power must be out in this area… how am I going to find the bed-and-breakfast?"

A pair of headlights appeared behind Patricia's SUV and then blue and red lights began flashing and whining into the night. Patricia looked into the outside mirror and saw a cop car almost on her bumper. She rolled her eyes and eased to a stop. A minute later a young officer stepped out into the storm and approached the driver's side door. Patricia rolled down her window. "Saw you take the turnoff," the cop called out over the howling winds. "Saw your license plate. Are you lost?"

Patricia looked up into a handsome face that took her off guard. But the face also seemed filled with a hardness that made her feel uncomfortable. She had expected to see an older, overweight cop, not a young man who reminded her of a daring soldier in an old war movie. "I'm due at a bed-and-breakfast that's located at 181 Shadow Lane. My GPS quit working," she explained.

"181 Shadow Lane?" the cop asked and then shook his head against the winds. "You must mean the old North place."

"I…guess. I mean, if that's the bed-and-breakfast." Patricia reached into her purse and pulled out an address book. "Yes, the place I'm due at is located at 181 Shadow Lane."

"Yeah, I wouldn't call the old North place a bed-and-breakfast…more like a nightmare," the cop said, looking doubtful. He then introduced himself. "My name is Gary Horne. What's your name?"

"Uh…Patricia McKay," Patricia stammered, shocked when the officer suddenly become personal. No "Officer," just "Gary Horne." "I'm a travel writer on assignment. I'm here to write about the B and B."

"Well, Patricia," Gary said, seemingly unaware of the cold, "the storm watch we were under has now turned into a warning. We're about to be pounded with some major wind and snow. Power is already out in this part of town. You better follow me and I'll drive you out to the old North place. Drive slow and drive careful. Winds are really picking up."

"I…okay, thanks…I'll drive carefully." Patricia rolled up her window and waited for Gary to get back into his patrol car and then take the lead. She eased off the brake and followed a pair of glowing headlights that led her through a dark, creepy town and that eventually turned into a very spooky countryside that, unbeknownst to Patricia, was lined with countless graveyards.

Patricia kept checking the gas gauge. Her SUV was now down to a quarter of a tank. "If we don't arrive soon I may be walking," she worried, following Gary at a slow crawl. To her relief, about half an hour later—what in normal weather would have only been a few minutes—Gary turned down a long dirt driveway that was covered with pristine snow. Patricia followed and didn't stop until the headlights attached to her SUV splashed onto a large, creepy manor that reminded her of a funeral home.

She gulped. "I guess this is it."

Gary jumped out of his patrol car and ran up to the SUV. Patricia reluctantly rolled down the window, flinching against the frigid wind.

"Not many people visit this old place," Gary said. "Rumors are an insane killer built it…don't know if that's true or not. All I know is that this place had been sitting empty since 1974. Not sure why the Graves bought this place. They're not even locals." Gary had to holler over the howling winds to make sure Patricia could hear him. "Anyway…if you encounter any trouble, just give the police a call and I'll come running."

"I…sure. I'll definitely do that," Patricia said.

Gary tipped his black police hat at Patricia, ran back to his car, jumped in, and drove away, leaving Patricia staring at a spooky manor that seemed filled with sleeping nightmares that were slowly beginning to wake up.

chapter two

Hauling two frozen suitcases into a spooky manor that was now dressed up as a creepy bed-and-breakfast wasn't an easy task, but Patricia managed to complete the chore without freezing to death.

"Goodness, that wind is enough to cut me in half," she complained, stepping into a large front room that, to her dismay, resembled a funeral parlor that looked as if it had been pulled from some cheesy 1950s B-rated horror movie. A dark red curtain separated the room into two sections. A wooden desk, acting as a check-in station, sat beyond the curtain, surrounded by dark green walls holding stained glass windows that were enough to creep out any sensible mind.

"Hello?" Patricia called out. "Is anyone here?"

A head popped around the curtain before Patricia could say another word. The head was attached to a stick. "No one here but us chickens," the head spoke and then chuckled. Patricia nearly screamed. But then a man who appeared to be sixty years old stepped out from behind the curtain holding a stick that the head was attached to. "Patricia McKay?"

"I…oh…yes." Patricia nodded, grateful to see a living person—even if the living person was dressed like a mortician. "You must be Mr. Graves?"

"My real name is Ben Grands, but I changed it to Graves just to add a little spice," Ben explained and then lowered the stick he was holding. "Charles and I like to joke around at times, isn't that right, Charles?" The head attached to the stick, a very realistic head, said: "Yeah, we like to have a few laughs."

"You're a ventriloquist," Patricia quickly pointed out, staring into a thin face that held a silver mustache.

"Used to be, yes," Ben said, nodding. "My wife and I traveled the world working one show after the next. We retired last year after I had a mild stroke. All better now."

"I'm glad to hear that," Patricia replied in a sincere voice even though she felt completely spooked by the realistic head. "Is your wife around, Mr. Grands…uh…Graves?"

"No, afraid not. Melinda traveled to Michigan to see her sister a few days ago. Poor Lila took ill again. That makes, oh, a million times the poor dear has taken ill this year," Ben explained, not bothering to hide his sarcasm.

"A million and one," the head added.

"Oh yes, a million and one, Charlie."

"I…hope your sister-in-law will be okay," Patricia told Ben. "By the way, how do you have electricity?" she asked, having just now realized the lights were on.

"Oh, I invested in a top-of-the-line generator," Ben replied. "We're way out in the country, lots of winter snowstorms—I knew it would come in handy."

"Good thinking," Patricia said as she looked around. "I would like to get checked in if that's all right. It's been a very tiring day."

"Of course." Ben smiled and carried the head and stick he was holding over to the wooden desk. "Melinda does all the administrative stuff, but I guess I should at least ask you to sign your name in the guest registry book."

Patricia dropped her eyes down onto a heavy red book that looked to be an antique. It reminded of her something she would see in an old western hotel that was lost in time. She put down the two suitcases she was holding and watched Ben open the book. To her surprise she spotted five other guest names. "There are more guests here? I assumed I was the only one. I didn't see any other vehicles outside."

"I had everyone park out back," Ben explained as Patricia signed the guest book. "There is a small but convenient concrete parking area back there. I can move your vehicle for you if you want."

Patricia looked into Ben's face. Although creepy in appearance, almost replicating Vincent Price, the eccentric man appeared harmless. "My SUV is parked just out front and is very low on gas," she explained.

"No worries, I won't go for a joy ride," Ben promised.

Patricia smiled and handed over the keys to her SUV. "What room am I in, Mr. Grands...uh—"

"Just call me Ben."

"Okay." Patricia smiled again. "What room will I be in?"

Ben took the keys to Patricia's SUV and then slowly folded his arms. "I'm afraid you're in room eight," he told Patricia in a voice that suddenly became very solemn. "I understand that you are here to put the Dead and Breakfast on the map, and even write out a murder mystery for our guests to enjoy. However, I feel that before you begin working there are a few facts that you should be made aware of."

Patricia felt her heart sink. "I'm all ears, Ben," she said, dreading what she would hear.

Ben walked Patricia over to a cobblestone fireplace that was holding a warm fire. The fireplace appeared very old and...sour...rather than warm and welcoming. Patricia walked across the funeral home–style rug that covered the old hardwood floor.

"What did your boss tell you about the Dead and Breakfast?" Ben asked.

"Nothing solid, I'm afraid," Patricia replied. "It does seem that my boss, Edna, did a little more research after I left—or maybe she knew a lot more than she let on before I left; that's more likely, knowing Edna. I know very little about this B and B and very little about Whispering Hills. The last time we spoke, just a little while ago, Edna did tell me that some murders have taken place in Whispering Hills. My suspicion is those murders are somehow tied to this…manor." Patricia walked her eyes around the gloomy room and then shook her head. "That's all I know."

Ben nodded. "Let me give you a little bit of the history of the place. In 1867, after the Civil War ended, a man by the name of Henry Graves—Graves truly being his last name— left his home in South Carolina and moved to Ohio to marry a woman by the name of Veronica Drakes. Henry Graves, according to the history books, fought very bravely for the Confederate Army and left his home very bitter, claiming General Lee deliberately allowed his troops to lose at Gettysburg in order to lose the war."

"Why would a man like that leave his home to marry a woman from the north?" Patricia asked, hearing the storm winds screaming and howling outside in the dark night.

"Ah," Ben said and held up a patient finger. "Henry Graves had revenge on his mind. Allow me to explain." Ben lowered his finger. "Henry Graves did leave his home—but only after he was forced to leave by certain officials who did not like him writing long, intelligent articles claiming General Lee turned traitor. You see, the South could have won the war…but that's for another time." Ben placed his hands behind his back and continued. "Henry managed to romance the daughter of a powerful politician. In time Henry was allowed into the political arena, and that's when he began sabotaging his enemies…men connected to army officials who talked General Lee into betraying the South…or so Henry Graves claimed."

"Ben, whether any of this is true or not, the Civil War has

been over for many, many decades and even now our country is still healing from that ugly wound," Patricia pointed out.

"I agree," Ben said, "but please allow me to continue." Patricia hesitated and then nodded. "Henry's agenda was discovered and certain men were sent to this very manor to kill him. Henry found out and…sadly…killed his wife and then took his own life, knowing by doing so he would mortally wound the heart of the man he believed controlled General Lee. Afterward the manor was boarded up and left empty until 1974, when a man by the name of Griffin North bought it and began extensive renovations."

"Is there a story behind that?" Patricia asked.

Ben nodded. "Griffin North was related to Henry Graves."

"How?" Patricia asked, feeling her curiosity reluctantly waking up.

"Veronica Drakes had a son before she was killed," Ben explained. "In order to protect the child Veronica's father renamed him and then sent the boy away." Ben glanced down at the fire. "Griffin North turned this manor into a nursing home until 1994. Why? No one really knows. In 1994 the man died of a sudden heart attack and was found dead in…room eight." Patricia winced. "Afterward the state shut down the nursing home and the manor has been empty ever since."

"Until now," Patricia pointed out.

"Turns out Griffin North is my old man…never knew him, though. My mother divorced Griffin when I was very young," Ben confessed, and Patricia's eyes widened. "A few years ago, when my mother died, I was contacted by a lawyer who told me all about this manor. It seems that Griffin left the manor to my mother. I have no idea why. Anyway, my mother, whom I was never really close to, decided to hand the manor over to me when she died. Of course, I'm sixty years old now…would have been nice if dear old mother would have handed this manor over to me sooner. But late is better than never."

Patricia stared into Ben's thin face. "So you…took the past and used it to create a spooky bed-and-breakfast?" she asked.

Ben nodded. "Working as a ventriloquist paid the bills, but my profession certainly didn't make me rich. And sadly, because my wife and I are childless, I don't have a legacy to leave anyone. So, I decided to do something very…radical…dramatic…and turn a cursed heritage into a funny joke…one last joke."

"I'm afraid I don't understand," Patricia confessed. "What does turning the manor into a creepy funeral home have to do with your heritage or a joke?"

Ben slowly raised his eyes. "People love to be scared," he explained. "I enjoy a good scare myself. When I inherited this manor, I decided to turn fear into a joke…anger into fun…rage into silliness." Ben sighed. "I've always felt cursed," he told Patricia in a sad voice. "I've always felt as if a curse was chasing me all my life. When I discovered the truth after Mother died, I understood why. For a while, I was filled with a great deal of anger and rage, but then I decided, because I am a comedian after all, to get the last laugh on Henry Graves because it all began with him."

Patricia felt Ben was leaving out a few facts. First, he claimed his last name was Grands—but the man his mother had been married to was named Griffin North, whom she divorced. Maybe she remarried? Patricia wanted to question Ben but her mind was teetering on the verge of complete exhaustion. *I'll give Ben the third degree tomorrow,* Patricia promised herself and then reached down to pick up her suitcases. As she did a beautiful woman with deep black hair entered the room.

"Oh, hello, Lara," Ben stated and quickly offered a curious eye. "Up for a little midnight snack?"

The woman glanced at Patricia and then focused back on Ben. "It's not even nine o'clock, Uncle Ben. Save the chocolate cake for after midnight."

"Deal," Ben agreed and then nodded at Patricia. "Lara Braceton, meet Patricia McKay, the travel writer who is going to make the Dead and Breakfast famous...and write real facts."

"Hello," Patricia said as she studied Lara. She was very beautiful, but Patricia had to admit her dress code was a little...nerdy. Lara was dressed in an unflattering green and orange polka-dotted dress. Also, the poor girl was wearing thick glasses that covered a pair of beautiful blue eyes.

"Hello," Lara said in a happy voice. "Ben told me a writer was due to arrive." Lara hurried over to Patricia on excited legs. "There's no internet here. I couldn't research you, but from what Ben told me, you come highly recommended. So, tell me...what are some of your books? Maybe I've read them. Of course, I don't recognize the name Patricia McKay, but you probably write under a different name. I know I would in the crazy world we're forced to live in."

"Uh...well, I haven't written any books. I'm a travel writer. I travel the world writing...well, humor pieces for a travel magazine," Patricia explained and then winced a little. "Sorry to disappoint you."

Lara shrugged. "I work in a school cafeteria back in Los Angeles, so don't feel too bad." she said.

"You're from LA? What are you doing in Ohio...and... here?" Patricia motioned around at the creepy front room.

"Because I dig spooky stories." Lara beamed. "You see, I want to write my first book and when Aunt Melinda told me all about this manor and what Uncle Ben was planning to do, I knew my train had finally arrived." Lara walked her excited eyes around. "A creepy history...murder...mystery, and tragedy. All the elements a writer needs to write a bestselling book!"

"So, you see, you're not the only one who is going to write about this manor...or shall we say...about the Dead and Breakfast," Ben informed Patricia in a voice that didn't exactly sound pleased. "My niece is going to focus her book entirely on this manor." Ben looked at Lara with a wary eye. "We need all the publicity we can get, right?"

"I need a bestselling book," Lara pointed out. She locked eyes with Patricia and smiled. "I've spent weeks studying the history of this manor. I probably know more than Uncle Ben. I'm going to write a bestseller and make this place famous! Of course, I might change a few details to add a little spice to the mix." Lara scanned the room again, ignoring Ben's low sigh. "I know I could have chosen some place closer to home. For instance, a chain of mystery bed-and-breakfasts are opening in Oregon—"

"Don't remind me," Patricia groaned.

Lara shrugged. "I need something that is real…tangible… potent. Something my readers can latch their teeth onto and see with their own eyes. After all, I don't plan to work in a school cafeteria my entire life. Lara Braceton is going to make a name for herself."

"I…hope you do," Patricia told Lara, feeling a certain connection to the woman. Lara was sincere in her passion to write a great murder mystery novel, and that was admirable. Patricia recalled when she was a young, struggling writer herself. "Well, it's been a long day. I've had a very long drive."

"Room eight awaits," Ben told Patricia and then made the head talk: "Room eight awaits."

Patricia sighed. "Isn't there another room?"

"I can change rooms with you," Lara blurted out.

"No," Ben snapped in a quick tone that startled Patricia. "I've already told you no."

Lara made a pouty face. "A murder took place in your room and I'm banned."

Patricia looked at Ben with rather curious eyes. For a brief second, she felt as if Ben had somehow…trapped her into staying in room eight for some an unknown, deep, hidden reason. "Uh…before I turn in for the night, may I ask who the other guests are, Ben?"

Ben shrugged. "Just people who…showed up in the storm," he said and then held up the keys to Patricia's SUV. "I better go move your SUV." Ben reached into his pocket, pulled out another key, handed it to Patricia, and smiled. "The key to your room."

Patricia watched Ben leave the room and then turned to look at Lara. Lara smiled. "I'll help you carry your luggage to your room. What Uncle Ben doesn't know won't hurt him."

Patricia was too tired to say no.

Patricia walked down a long, creepy hallway whose floor creaked with every step. The hall was lined with numerous closed doors. "This is one place I'm never going to visit again," she told Lara, dragging her tired feet down the hallway, walking past one closed door after another. "There are only five other guests, Lara. Why am I assigned to the creepy murder room?"

"Some of these doors lead into rooms that are off-limits," Lara explained, carrying one of Patricia's suitcases. "This manor has a lot of scary, hidden secrets."

Patricia glanced over at Lara. "And why am I the one who has to stay in the creepy murder room? You actually want to stay in there but your uncle won't let you."

Lara shrugged her shoulders. "Uncle Ben is a strange man; that's all I can say."

"Or maybe he's not so strange?"

"What?" Lara asked in a confused voice.

"Nothing," Patricia replied and fought back a yawn. She continued down the shadowy hallway and stopped in front of a thick wooden door that had the number 8 carved into it. "Well, I guess this is my room."

"Let's go inside," Lara pleaded. "I want to see what it looks like."

"Sure." Patricia set down her suitcase, glanced up the silent hallway, and then used the key Ben gave her to unlock the room door. "I...well, no sense in standing out here all night," she told Lara and reluctantly pushed the door open. Lara didn't wait. She pushed past Patricia and burst into the room. "Lara...wait!" Patricia hurried into the room after her and immediately slid to a stop. "Oh my," she gasped.

"Oh my is right...wow!" Lara exclaimed.

Patricia stood frozen, standing in complete shock. This wasn't what she expected at all in this creepy building. The room that stood before her wasn't decorated like a spooky funeral room. Rather, it was designed with amazing riches and spectacular delicacies. A large bed stood in the middle of room decorated with a red silk bed curtain. Hand-carved furnishings that must have cost a fortune were placed along burgundy walls on which hung lavish paintings. All of the decor complemented the lovely, expensive, hardwood floor that seemed to glow. The room, it appeared, had been designed to fit a queen. But what caught Patricia's attention the most was not the lavish setting...but dust. The room was caked with dust.

"It's like no one has been inside this room for years and years," Patricia whispered, feeling a deep mystery begin clawing at her mind.

"Look at all this dust." Lara whistled and ran her right finger across an antique nightstand perched beside the bed. "Looks like Aunt Melinda and Uncle Ben skipped cleaning this room. But why?" Lara turned to Patricia. "I think Uncle Ben is holding out on me. I'm going to go and talk to him."

Patricia didn't know what to say. Exhaustion was

torturing her mind. "Go easy, Lara. I'm sure Ben has his reasons."

"Reasons I intend to bring into the light," Lara assured Patricia. She threw her eyes around the room and then marched away, leaving Patricia all alone.

"What a day…what a night," Patricia spoke aloud and then, after retrieving her luggage, reluctantly closed the door. Silence gripped the room. But why? Surely the storm winds should have been heard screaming and howling outside. Patricia eased over to the window and pulled back the heavy red drapes. "What?" she gasped, seeing wood instead of glass. "This window has been boarded over. Who on earth did that?"

Turning away from the window, Patricia quickly scanned the room. According to Ben, a murder had taken place in the room…but where? "Why did you send me to this room, Ben? What do you want me to know—or discover?" Patricia's eyes locked on the door, and for a few seconds she considered leaving. But then she reminded her frightened heart that she was a logical, brave woman who didn't scare easily. "I've survived worse than this. I mean, for crying out loud, I survived Paris. I'm not going to let this room scare me. It's just a room…a very strange room, but just a room." Patricia walked her eyes around. "A room without a bathroom, I see," she sighed and then dropped her head down. "Perfect ending to a perfect day."

Feeling far too tired to remain scared, Patricia pulled back the bed curtain and looked down at a bed that was caked with dust. A thick brownish red blanket covered the bed; a blanket that was designed with curious little flowers that Patricia couldn't identify.

"Why did they not bother to clean the room before I arrived?" Patricia wondered aloud. "I can't sleep on this bed. I think I'll…" Patricia turned away from the bed and spotted a green couch perched in the far corner. "Bingo. Now all I have to do is find the bathroom, brush my teeth, and get some sleep. I have a bad feeling tomorrow is going to be a very trying day. But first..." Patricia went for her purse, found a sleepy cell phone, and called Brian. Brian picked up on the first ring. "I'm all settled in, safe and sound," she told him, grateful to hear his voice.

"Tried calling a few times," Brian said. "Weather report is claiming that there is a bad winter storm in your area. I was worried."

"My cell phone lost service and then my GPS went out," Patricia complained as she walked her eyes around the room and then decided to sit down on the green couch. "Brian, you wouldn't believe the spooky story I'm trapped in. Remind me to punch Edna in the nose when I get home."

"That bad, huh?" Brian asked. He reached across a tired work desk and grabbed a chocolate donut.

"Bad isn't the word. I'm currently sitting in a room full of dust and where a murder supposedly happened."

"A murder?" Brian asked in a concerned tone.

"Decades ago," Patricia assured Brian. "It's a long story. I'm too tired to go into what details I know. I wanted to call you and let you know I'm safe before going to sleep."

"I'm glad you did," Brian replied. "I called Edna and she told me you called her, so I figured you'd call me when you could. But I have to admit when I couldn't get ahold of you, I was ready to get in my truck and drive to Ohio and start looking for you."

Patricia smiled. Brian was sweet. "Well, I'm safe," she said and then yawned. "Brian, I need to locate a bathroom and then get some sleep. I'll call you in the morning, okay?"

"Call me past noon. I have to pull a late night and then go crash myself. State has really been breathing down my neck today, but I managed to make a few ugly politicians take a step back." Brian took a bite of his donut. "Don't forget to say your prayers, okay?"

"I won't," Patricia promised and then said good night to Brian. After putting her cell phone away, she fished out a wash towel, a toothbrush, a tube of toothpaste, and then left the room and stepped back out into the creepy hallway. "Now…which room is the bathroom?"

Before Patricia could begin her search, a door opened. Patricia paused and watched a handsome young man who looked to be about her age step out into the hallway wearing a dark gray suit. The man spotted Patricia and quickly offered a polite wave. "I…you wouldn't know where the bathroom is, would you?" Patricia asked.

"That door." The man pointed to a closed door across the hallway and then looked back at Patricia, noticing what a beautiful woman she was. "Did you just arrive?" he asked.

"Yes." Patricia nodded. "I'm a travel writer here to write a piece on this…uh…bed-and-breakfast."

"Oh, a travel writer…cool." The man eased close to Patricia and smiled. "My name is Foster Carlton."

"I'm Patricia McKay," Patricia said as she studied Foster's face. Foster resembled a beach volleyball player. What in the world was a guy like him doing in a spooky manor like this in the middle of a snowstorm? "Well, it's been a long day. I need to brush my teeth and turn in."

Foster nodded. "I understand. I was just about to go outside. I forgot my laptop battery charger in my Jeep. Maybe I'll see you tomorrow morning at breakfast."

"Maybe—" Patricia began to reply but stopped when a horrible scream pierced the hallway. Patricia immediately guessed who the scream might belong to. "Lara!" she yelled, dropping her belongings and dashing down the hallway. Foster followed.

Patricia hurried down the L-shaped staircase lined with red carpet and then ran back into the front room. And there, to her horror, lying on the floor, was Lara. When Foster spotted Lara, he slid to a stop.

"Hey...someone stabbed her...there's a knife...her back...."

Vulnerability and fear gripped Patricia's heart. She ran her eyes to the curtain dividing the room. It was moving. The front door was open and icy air was attacking the curtain. The killer, it appeared, had escaped out into the storm.

"Call nine-one-one!" she yelled at Foster and then carefully bent down and examined the dead woman. "Oh, Lara...no," she moaned, immediately knowing that Lara was...dead.

Foster ran to the front desk and snatched up a black phone. "Hey...I think the phone is dead. I can't get a dial tone."

"Use your cell phone!"

"It's in my room!" Foster spun away from the desk and charged back upstairs, leaving Patricia all alone with Lara.

"Oh, Lara, you poor girl," Patricia moaned as tears began falling from her eyes. "You had your entire life ahead of you." Patricia quickly wiped at her tears and used the time she had alone to examine Lara. First, she examined her hands. "Oh. You were fighting with someone. Your fingernails are broken." Next, Patricia checked the woman's arms and neck. "Scratches on your arms...bruises on your neck." Patricia stared into the distance. "Whoever killed you didn't do it easily; good for you," she whispered as tears began to flow again.

"What is—?" a voice yelled in horror. Patricia shot her head up and saw Ben standing near the front door. "Lara...is this a joke?"

"Someone stabbed her," Patricia explained in a weak, sick voice. "I'm so sorry, Mr. Grands...Ben. Your niece is...dead."

"What? No...this is a joke...no!" Ben ran to Lara's body, bent down, and touched the murder weapon. "This is a real knife. It's a kitchen knife." Ben's eyes grew large with fright. "That's...real blood."

Patricia nodded sadly. "Someone stabbed Lara and then ran out into the storm. The front door was wide open when I got down here."

"But...I just came from outside. I found the front door open, but I know I closed it when I went out. I didn't see anyone," Ben insisted as anger flashed through his voice. "Who would want to kill this innocent girl? Why, she's never hurt anyone a day in her life! My niece was...annoying, yes, but she was harmless and...innocent!"

I'm trapped in a real-life game of Clue, Patricia thought as she stared into Ben's angry eyes. "One of the guests...a man named Foster...went to call for help. He tried to use the phone sitting on that desk over there but said there wasn't a dial tone."

Ben shot to his feet, ran to the desk, and grabbed the phone. "There...isn't a dial tone," he confirmed and slammed the receiver down. "What's going on?"

Patricia lowered her eyes and studied Lara's hands. "Maybe Lara was killed for a reason, Ben," she stated in a miserable voice. "Maybe she was killed because somebody didn't want her writing a certain book?"

"But...but...." Ben ran a pair of shaky hands through his gray hair. "It's the curse," he stammered. "It's always been the curse! I tried to get the last laugh, but...Henry got the last laugh on me." Patricia looked up at Ben and saw all the color drain from his face. "Henry got...the last laugh. The curse...I couldn't kill it," he whispered in a frail voice and then simply sat down behind the desk and put his hands over his tearful face.

"I called nine-one-one!" Foster's urgent voice came bursting down the stairs. "They're on their way!"

Patricia raised her eyes and watched Foster run back into the room. "Please go find a sheet to cover the body," she pleaded. When Foster hesitated, she asked, "What is it?"

"Someone killed that woman," Foster said and then

turned to Ben. "What kind of place are you running here?" he yelled. "A woman is dead and you're sitting there with your hands over your face."

"Leave me alone, Mr. Carlton," Ben warned in an angry tone. "That's my niece who was killed. If you want a refund that's fine. You can leave anytime you want."

"No one can leave," Patricia countered in a stern tone. "The police will need to question everyone." With those words Patricia stood up and walked over to Ben. Without saying a word, she carefully glanced down at his hands. Ben had not put on a pair of gloves before going outside to drive her SUV to the back of the manor. His hands were red from the cold but clear of any signs of a struggle…blessedly clear.

"I'll be right back." Patricia turned away from the desk and walked to the front door, staring down at the floor the entire way. Only one set of snow tracks were on the floor. "Ben's tracks from when he came in from the snow, which means the killer didn't come in from the snow," she murmured. "The killer was already inside."

Patricia returned her eyes back to Ben. "What are you doing?" Foster asked, watching Patricia examine the room.

"Looking around," Patricia responded in a distant voice. It was clear that Foster wasn't the killer because the man had been standing with her when Lara was killed. But who was Foster? What was he doing at the bed-and-breakfast? Patricia would find out. But for the time being, she needed to examine the room Lara had been killed in. "Ben, are there any hidden hallways in this manor?"

"What?" Ben raised his head. "I…not that I'm aware of. This is a very old manor, so I guess it's possible. I don't know."

Patricia continued to walk around the room and then slowly made her way back to Ben. "It's time you called the other guests downstairs. If anyone is missing, we might know who our killer is." She then looked over at Foster and noticed he tensed up. Why? *Looks like I'm trapped in another murder case. Looks like I'm cursed as well,* Patricia thought and then locked her eyes on Lara's body. *Don't worry, Lara, I'm going to find out who killed you…even if it means I put my life in danger trying.*

chapter three

Gary Horne pulled back the white sheet and looked at Lara's body with eyes that were, to Patricia's anger, full of distaste rather than compassion.

"I knew something like this was going to happen," he fussed to no one in particular—the no one in particular crowd consisting of Patricia, Ben, and four other guests who were standing in a tight group close to the check-in desk. "Ever since I was a kid, I've known this place was cursed." Gary shot a hard eye up at Ben. "Can't understand why you would want to turn this place into some kind of freak attraction."

Ben's face was pale. He felt sick. "My niece has been killed. I will not stand here and tolerate insults," he warned Gary. "You have run your mouth to me before young man. If you continue to harass me, I will contact my attorney and then report you to your superior."

"Sure, sure," Gary replied in a sarcastic tone as he covered Lara's body up. "Play innocent while a woman is dead. That's the way it always is." Gary brushed his hands and then stood up. He looked directly at Patricia. "Looks like you got to the show just in time, huh?"

"No," Patricia answered in a cold voice that pushed Gary back. "Murder is never an attraction, Officer Horne."

Gary frowned. Patricia was a cutie but her attitude wasn't so attractive. Oh well. That's the way the ball game played out sometimes. "Well, Chief Winchester is on his way, so everyone sit tight until he gets here. In the meantime, I'll just ask a few questions." Gary tried to speak in a tough, authoritative tone but ended up sounding like a real jerk. "I want to know where everyone was when Lara Braceton was killed…beginning with…you." Gary pointed at Foster.

Foster was standing close to a man named Toby Ells, nervously chewing on his thumb nail. "I was upstairs with Ms. McKay," he told Gary and then glanced at Toby. Toby nodded.

"You seem really nervous," Gary pointed out. "Keep eating at your thumb and you'll end up having four fingers."

"I'm nervous because a woman is dead and a killer is loose and I believe we are all in danger," Foster snapped at Gary, looking defiant. He stopped biting his thumb nail and pointed toward the front door. "The sooner we get out of here the better."

"In this storm…no way," Gary snapped back. He slowly lowered his hand down onto a black utility belt that was wrapped around his waist and touched what appeared to be a Glock 17. "No one is leaving here tonight…storm or no storm. Is that clear?"

Foster's eyes filled with rage. "We're not prisoners. Everyone is innocent until proven—"

"Don't feed me that line," Gary plowed into Foster. "A woman is dead, so spare me the line about being innocent. As of right now everyone standing in this room is guilty in my eyes until proven innocent. In other words, you're all suspects." Gary glared at Toby. "You've been really quiet, mister."

Toby narrowed a pair of dark eyes that worried—and scared—Patricia. The man appeared to be in his early fifties but looked as healthy as a twenty-year-old. He stood tall and powerful, hovering over Foster like a giant. "I've called my attorney. I've been advised to remain silent," he spoke in a voice that sent a chill down Patricia's spine.

Gary rolled his eyes then looked at the expensive gray suit Toby was wearing—a suit that was very similar to the suit Foster was wearing. "Nice suit…looks like it cost you a few paychecks. Mind if I ask what you do for a living?"

To Patricia's relief Gary, the idiot cop, actually asked a sensible question. "Mr. Ells is an archaeology professor," Foster said. "He teaches at—"

Toby quickly cleared his throat and shot a hard eye at Foster. Foster winced and looked down at his feet. "I'm a college professor," Toby informed Gary in a flat tone.

Gary's mind didn't compute the information the way a skilled detective would. The guy just nodded and moved his eyes to a lovely woman named Karan Radoslav. "What's your story?" he asked, clearly showing no interest in a woman who looked to be about Toby's age. Sure, Karan was a very pretty woman with short blond hair and obviously had good taste in clothing—but makeup could only do so much to hide age.

"I've already told you," Karan informed Gary in an icy tone. "My name is Karan Radoslav. I live in California. I research—"

"Spooks…yeah, you told me," Gary cut Karan off. He rolled his eyes and said, "They come out of the woodwork… bunch of nuts."

"I don't appreciate your insult," Karan fired at Gary and then threw her arms over a lovely blue sweater that almost looked as if it were made of silk instead of wool. "I have a very distinguished reputation. I also have a master's degree from Yale—"

"Those colleges are run by tyrants who think man-made degrees make a person smart," Gary plowed into Karan. "I could care less if you had ten degrees." Gary pointed down at Lara's body. "A woman is dead. That's all that matters tonight." Gary turned his attention to a woman who appeared to be Patricia's age. "You said your name was Susie Baker, right?"

Susie Baker nodded. "Lara was…my best friend. She talked me into driving to Ohio with her," she confessed through teary eyes. "I can't believe someone killed her. Why? Lara never hurt anyone. She was so kind and…well, a little strange, but she had a sweet heart to her."

Patricia stared at Susie. The woman was a little plump around the edges and, sadly, wasn't very pretty. She looked like the type of woman who carried a knife in her back—a knife in the form of low self-esteem. The poor girl looked as if she were ready to crawl into a grave and cover herself up. "You and Lara were good friends?"

Susie nodded. "The best," she confirmed and then quickly glanced down at the floor. "Lara introduced me to the man I was going to marry."

Gary made a "you, get married?" face. Susie was wearing a baggy green and white dress that didn't complement her face or her short black hair. All Gary saw was a plump donut that needed to go on a diet. "Did you ever have a reason to want to kill your friend?" he asked.

"What?" Susie cried out. "You must be joking! I loved Lara. She and I were closer than sisters!"

Patricia watched Susie's chubby cheeks turn red and sighed. *Should have listened to the old couple back at that Denny's,* she thought. "Calm down," she told Susie and then threw her eyes at Gary. "There's a way to question people, Officer Horne."

"And you're an expert?" Gary asked in a sarcastic tone.

"I've…dealt with my share of murders in the past, so yes," Patricia confessed and then immediately regretted her words. Fatigue was eating away at her mind—a mind that felt as if it were crumbling into sharp little pieces of misery.

"Oh really?" Gary asked and then slapped his arms over a black and blue police coat. "Are you a cop too?"

"No," Patricia confirmed. She let out a miserable breath. "I'm a travel writer, Officer Horne."

Gary shook his head. "How does a travel writer get involved with murder?"

"I...murder just seems to be around." Patricia made a painful face. Her statement sounded pathetic and stupid.

"Maybe you like murder, huh? Maybe murder gives your writing more...flavor?" Gary asked in an accusing voice.

Patricia wanted to slap the guy but resisted. In all truth she couldn't blame the jerk for accusing her. If Patricia were in Gary's shoes, she knew she would probably consider a strange travel writer who was always involved with murder a suspect as well. "Time will tell, I guess," she answered in a way that took Gary aback. "Everyone standing here is marked with guilt in your eyes. All we can do is prove our innocence, right?"

Gary narrowed his eyes. "Yeah...something like that," he said and then stopped talking when the front door banged open. A short, plump man with a round belly trudged into the front room shaking snow off a brown coat. "Chief—"

"What is this about, Gary?" Chief Winchester barked in a rough voice. "Why was I called away from my home to come to this cursed place?"

Gary pointed down at the white sheet covering Lara's body. "We have a murder, Chief."

Chief Winchester spotted the white sheet, bent down, snatched the sheet back, studied Lara's body, and then shook his head with disgust. "Call Joe. Tell him to get out here and get this body," he barked at Gary and then covered Lara's body back up.

"Got it," Gary said. He hurried toward the staircase, pulling out a black cell phone.

Chief Winchester stood up and eyed Ben. "I'm shutting this place down for good. Is that clear?"

"My attorney may say otherwise," Ben replied, feeling far too weak and sick to his stomach to argue. "My niece has been killed, but that doesn't mean I'm going to lose every cent I invested in this bed-and-breakfast—"

"Bed-and-breakfast my foot!" Chief Winchester yelled. "A bed-and-breakfast is a cozy two-story house that sits out in the country surrounded by a pretty lake or something. This place is an old, cursed manor that should have been torn down decades ago!" Chief Winchester shook his head and then focused on Patricia. "The Dead and Breakfast—that's what that guy is going to call this cursed place. Can you believe that?"

"Yes," Patricia said, nodding. "Uh…Chief Winchester, my name is Patricia McKay. I'm a travel writer from Atlanta who was sent to write a piece on the Dead and Breakfast. My boss wants to help Mr. Graves…uh, Mr. Grands, establish a popular reputation."

"Is that so?" Chief Winchester looked as if he wanted to vomit. He turned his attention to the other guests. "And who are all of you?" he barked.

One by one each guest stated their name. Chief Winchester listened with angry ears that were attached to a face that could have been the face of Mickey Rooney. "Listen to me," he ordered, yanking a brown muffler hat off his head, exposing a nearly bald head, "someone killed that young woman and I want answers. Until I get some answers no one is leaving. Is that clear?" Chief Winchester turned his attention to Gary. "Call Ralph when you get off the phone and get him out here…and wake up Reed while you're at it."

"Reed is on vacation, Chief. It's just me and Ralph working the night shifts…twelve-hour shifts…three on…two off…two on…three off—"

"I know the schedule!" Chief Winchester barked. "Just get Ralph out here."

"Ralph is sick, Chief, remember? I've been covering for him. As a matter of fact, tonight was Ralph's shift."

Chief Winchester kicked the floor. "Then wake up the day shift!"

"Melanie is sick, Chief. Trent has been pulling the day shift hours," Gary called out from the staircase. "Melanie has walking pneumonia."

"Is everyone sick?" Chief Winchester hollered.

"It's that time of year, Chief."

"I know that, Gary!" Chief Winchester kicked the floor again. "You just worry about getting the coroner out here, do you hear me!" Gary nodded. It was clear to Patricia the guy was used to Chief Winchester's temper. The chief turned to Ben. "I want to see the guest paperwork."

"Paperwork?" Ben asked in a confused voice.

"Yes, the guest paperwork. I want a copy of names, addresses, copies of driver's license—"

Ben reached down and picked up the guest registry book sitting on the check-in desk. "I had them sign in," he explained. "My wife, Melinda, usually handles all the paperwork, but she's away right now."

Chief Winchester squeezed his hands into two tight fists. "Surely you have a copy of their credit cards?"

"Each guest paid with cash and Ms. McKay is staying for free in exchange for writing an article about the bed-and-breakfast and creating a murder mystery script for me."

"A murder mystery script?" Chief Winchester threw his eyes at Patricia. "What in the world is Herman Munster talking about?"

Patricia didn't appreciate Chief Winchester insulting Ben, but what could she do? "Chief Winchester, perhaps you should call my boss. Edna should still be in her office. She works late hours."

"Yeah, maybe I should."

Patricia pulled a cell phone out of her coat pocket and called Edna. Edna picked up on the first ring. "What is it? What's wrong? Somethings wrong because the hair on the back of my neck has been standing up for the last couple of hours."

"A woman has been killed, Edna."

Edna quit pacing her office, froze in place, and made an "uh-oh" face. "You're not serious?"

"I'm...dead serious," Patricia confirmed. "Edna, I need you to speak to a man named Chief Winchester and explain to him why I was sent to Whispering Hills."

"Sure...okay, honey. Put the man on the phone."

Patricia held out her cell phone. "My boss."

Chief Winchester made a sour face and then snatched Patricia's phone away from her. "This is Chief Winchester..."

Patricia took a few steps back as Chief Winchester tore into Edna. She glanced at Toby and saw him glaring at Susie in a way that worried her. *What is a guy who majored in archaeology doing here?* her mind wondered. *And Foster...he seems like Toby's lap dog.* Toby felt Patricia looking at him and locked eyes with her in a way that told her to back off. Patricia quickly looked back at Chief Winchester. *Toby is bad news...real bad news. But is he the killer? He came downstairs with Karan and Susie. No snow was on his shoes.*

"Yeah, yeah, I get it," Chief Winchester plowed into Edna. "You sent your girl to write a silly article about a cursed place. Remind me to send you a thank you card!" Chief Winchester handed Patricia back her cell phone. "You're in the clear. Your boss is going to fax my office all the papers I need on you. But that doesn't mean the rest of you are in the clear. Is that...clear?" Chief Winchester yelled at everyone else.

"Coroner is on his way, Chief," Gary said, stepping back into the room.

"Good." Chief Winchester nodded. "In the meantime, everyone is hereby confined to your rooms. If I catch anyone out of their room you will be placed under immediate arrest. Is that clear?" Everyone simply nodded and walked back upstairs without saying a word. Patricia lingered for a few seconds but then decided to go upstairs and rest her weary mind.

It was going to be a very long night—and more than likely a very long day tomorrow.

"No, I'm not kidding," Patricia complained to Brian as she plopped down on the green couch. "I need you to please dig up as much as you can on the guest names I gave you. My gut is telling me that Toby guy is bad news."

"But you said he came downstairs with no snow on his shoes," Brian pointed out, struggling to clear his eyes of sleep. "How could he be the killer?"

"He could have changed his shoes. I don't know, I'm not sure...maybe he isn't?" Patricia confessed, walking her eyes around the lavish room that Ben had assigned her to. "I know Foster didn't kill Lara. Karan and Susie...they came downstairs with Toby. But Brian, what if the killer escaped out into the storm?"

"Could it be that Ben Graves is the killer?" Brian asked.

Patricia slowly closed her weary eyes. "That's the most logical explanation, isn't it?" she confessed in a miserable voice. "But I refuse to believe Mr. Graves...Grands... whatever he wants his last name to be...is a killer. I've looked into the man's eyes, Brian. He's strange and maybe even a little creepy brandishing that fake head of his around, but he's no killer. And he especially wouldn't kill his own niece."

"Then what?"

"The killer might have been wearing snow boots and

removed them before reentering the manor," Patricia suggested. "The killer could have come in through the back door or a basement door? This manor is pretty big. I haven't had a chance to explore the entire place, but from what I saw from the outside, this place is huge."

"Aren't bed-and-breakfasts usually—"

"Cozy and usually housed in a warm two-story home?" Patricia finished for Brian.

"Yeah."

"Well, let's just say the Dead and Breakfast isn't exactly...cozy," Patricia stated in a tired voice. "It's more like a nightmare. And to top it off, I'm assigned to a room that a murder supposedly happened in. Remind me to punch—"

"Edna in the nose when you get home. Yeah, you've already told me that," Brian told Patricia and then yawned. "Look, just stay in your room for the night and lock the door. I'm going to get a few winks and then fly up—"

"No!" Patricia exclaimed, surprised at the tone of her voice. "Brian...I know you mean well, but this is my case. I know you're a great cop, but there is a killer on the loose, and...well, if you run to my rescue, you may...get hurt."

"And you're in the clear?" Brian asked in a worried tone. "Seems to me that you could be the next target if your theory is right."

"My theory as to why Lara was killed?"

Brian nodded. "Maybe the killer overheard Lara claiming she was going to write a book full of hidden truths that maybe someone didn't want made public. If that's true—"

"I might be next because I was sent here to write a piece on this cursed place," Patricia finished for Brian.

"Exactly. So, I'm flying up."

Patricia sighed. The thought of Brian tangling with a devious creature like Toby put fear and dread into her heart. "I don't want you hurt, Brian. I love you."

"And I love you; that's why I'm coming up there," Brian whispered.

"Unfortunately, I just remembered we're in the midst of a huge storm. The airports are closed and the roads are closed too." Patricia saw Brian's worried face enter her exhausted mind. "You'll always be my hero, but right now I'm flying solo."

"You don't sound too disappointed."

"I'm grateful for this storm now because that means you're out of harm's way," Patricia explained in a tender voice. "Brian, you saved my life when that awful punk was trying to strangle me to death in that corn maze. I'll love you forever for that. Now let me return the favor. Please…stay home. Toby Ells puts a poison taste in my heart. The man is… vicious, Brian."

"I'm a cop, remember? I can handle criminals—"

"Brian, please," Patricia begged. "I looked into the eyes of this Toby guy; he's evil. He's not the type of guy who is scared of a cop. Let me handle this case…please."

"Do I have a choice?" Brian asked in a miserable voice. "Even if I wanted to get to you, I'm trapped until the storm in your area clears. Even then there's no telling how long it will be before the roads are cleared. I guess I should have realized that before saying I would fly up to you…guess I'm more tired than I thought."

"You're very concerned, Brian, that's all," Patricia said, struggling to soothe him. "Listen, I need you to find out as much as you can on the names I gave you, okay. That's how you can help me. In the meantime, I don't think Chief Winchester is going anywhere. Even if he does, that arrogant jerk Gary will most likely be assigned to hang around. I highly doubt the killer will strike twice in one night."

"You're probably right," Brian agreed and reached for a stale cup of coffee. "Just remember the gun I put in your purse."

"The Glock...yeah, I know. And...thank you, Brian."

Brian took a sip of coffee, closed his eyes, saw Patricia's beautiful face appear, and said, "Love you...sweet dreams," and then ended the call.

"Love you too," Patricia whispered and then dropped her cell phone down onto the couch. She sneezed from the dust, then closed her weary eyes and listened to the silence consuming the spooky room. "Why did you assign me this room, Ben? What do you want me to know?"

A low knock startled Patricia. Someone was standing outside in the hallway. Patricia jerked her eyes open and looked at the door. "Who is it?"

"Susie...we met downstairs. I'm...I was...Lara's best friend," a shaky voice answered. "I'm not supposed to be out of my room, but I need to talk to you. Please."

Patricia climbed to her feet as her eyes pierced the door. Was Susie the killer? Had the woman come to end Patricia's life? "She's not the killer," Patricia whispered, relying on her gut to speak the truth. "One second," she said louder.

Susie glanced down the spooky hallway and waited for Patricia to open the door. The hallway was silent. Gary and Chief Winchester were still downstairs with Ben. For the time being, she was in the clear. "Hurry."

Patricia unlocked and opened the door. She spotted a nervous face standing out in the hallway. "Come on inside."

Susie glanced down the hallway one last time and then brushed by Patricia on anxious legs. Patricia quickly closed and locked the room door. Susie heard Patricia activate the antique lock attached to the door and tensed up even more. The thought of being locked inside a room where Ben Graves had said a...murder had taken place was not very settling. Then again, a few minutes ago she had been standing in a room with an actual dead body.

"I'm very afraid to speak to you," Susie began, "but I just

have to speak to someone, and you…well, you seem to be okay. I heard Chief Winchester talking to your boss."

Patricia studied Susie's frightened face for a second and then calmly walked to the couch and plopped down. "You're scared that whoever killed Lara might try and kill you, right?"

Susie glanced around the creepy room and then nodded. "And I think I know who killed…Lara," she whispered as if a spider were crawling down her back. Susie eased over to the couch and lowered her voice. "Lara's uncle. He has to be the killer."

"Ben? Her uncle?" Patricia asked in a confused voice. "Why him?"

Susie clamped her hands together and locked down at the floor for a minute before speaking. "Ben is so…creepy. I overheard him telling Lara that he would do anything to put this silly bed-and-breakfast on the map." Susie raised her eyes. "Sure, Lara wanted to write a book about the history of this place… twist the story around a little…you know…write a good horror book. But Ben…he was practically ordering Lara what to write."

"And Lara disapproved?"

"Of course, she did," Susie exclaimed in a low whisper. "Susie's dream was to become a great author. I…well, I have to admit that Susie wasn't a very talented writer, but her heart was always in the right place. I always believed in supporting her—"

"And that's why you traveled to Ohio with her?" Patricia asked.

"Yes." Susie nodded and then shrugged. "Lara was my best friend and she always stood by me. Someone needed to stand by her, right?"

"I guess."

Patricia's noncommittal answer took Susie aback. "What is that supposed to mean?"

Patricia settled her weary mind. Susie wasn't a very difficult woman to figure out. Call it skill or experience or just plain old discernment, but Patricia had Susie's number. "Lara introduced you to a man you were *going* to marry. My guess is if you were still engaged to this person, you wouldn't be standing here."

Susie tensed up. "That's really none of your—"

"As much as you try to show remorse over Lara's death, I can't help but notice a little...relief in your eyes," Patricia continued. She slowly folded her arms together and narrowed her eyes a little. "When you mentioned that Lara introduced you to some man you were supposed to marry, I detected a little resentment. What happened, Susie? Did the man call off the wedding...or maybe end up falling in love with Lara?"

"You have a big mouth!" Susie snapped, looking like she regretted ever coming to Patricia's room.

"Maybe," Patricia agreed and quickly fought back a yawn. "All I'm trying to imply, Susie, is that you may not be as upset over Lara's death as you seem. The question is: Why?" Patricia furrowed her brow. "Also, why would you really follow Lara to Ohio if you were upset with her unless you wanted something bad to happen to her?"

"You're insane!"

"Maybe we should talk to Chief Winchester?" Patricia suggested.

All of the color stationed in Susie's chubby face fell down onto the old floor. "What? No!" she begged, changing her tone into that of a helpless victim. "I didn't kill Lara. For crying out loud, I came to your room to tell you who—"

"To point suspicion in the opposite direction?" Patricia asked. She unfolded her arms and stood up. "Susie, I looked into Ben's eyes. He isn't a killer. Creepy? Yes. Eccentric? Maybe. A killer? No. And Lara was his niece!"

"Then why did he send his wife away? Huh? Tell me

that," Susie begged. "And why did he call Lara and ask her to travel to Ohio? Huh? It's the perfect setup!"

"Maybe in your mind," Patricia informed Susie, "and maybe not. Maybe you were sent here to make me look left when I need to be looking right."

"What?" Susie gasped.

"Sister, I know a good act when I see one," Patricia told Susie in an exhausted voice. "I knew you were full of hot air when I opened my door and saw your face. You may have fooled Chief Winchester, but I'm a pro."

"I...I'm...out of here!" Susie marched to the door and began fiddling with the lock.

"Who sent you, Susie? Toby Ells?" Patricia asked as she watched Susie fumbling with the lock. "Karan Radoslav?"

"Leave me alone!" Susie snapped at Patricia, working desperately to disengage the old, rusty lock. "What's the matter with this thing?"

Patricia wanted to tell Susie to twist the lock left instead of right but used the time she had with the young woman to get some answers. "Who sent you, Susie? Answer me or I'm marching right downstairs and telling Chief Winchester that you killed Lara!"

Susie spun around. "What? I didn't kill Lara...I...."

"What?" Patricia approached Susie and pointed a hard finger at her. "Who sent you to my room, Susie? I want answers or else."

Susie stared into a pair of angry, stern, intelligent eyes that meant business. "Okay...okay," she whimpered, "I'll talk."

"Good." Patricia placed her hands on her hips and waited.

Susie struggled to gather her thoughts and then began to speak. "It's true. Lara introduced me to Mace, and I...fell in love with him," she told Patricia in a low, shaky voice. "Mace was so smart and funny. I couldn't believe he would like a chunky cookie like myself, but he did...he honestly did. Of course, Mace wasn't so skinny himself at the time."

"What happened?"

"Mace started hitting the gym. He shed his weight and got some muscles. Took him almost two years, but he became really fit, and then he joined a band and…wow, he became super popular like overnight." Susie let out a painful breath. "Mace began changing…and Lara started to take notice of him. She…stole him from me."

"Lara wasn't exactly a beauty queen. Pretty, yes…but a bit nerdy," Patricia pointed out.

"Yeah, but so what? Mace fell for her," Susie informed Patricia and then let her shoulders sag. "I never forgave her for stealing Mace…not that it mattered. Mace ended up dumping Lara and moving to Seattle. We both lost out."

Patricia felt a headache looming in the distance. "So why did you travel to Ohio with Lara?"

"To sabotage her book," Susie confessed. "When Lara told me her uncle was arranging for her to write a book that could make her famous, I knew my time to exact revenge had arrived. After all, I did all of Lara's editing for her. All I had to do was play along with her and let her write the book…and then sink her for good!" Susie looked into Patricia's eyes. "Lara asked me to accompany her here. If I had refused, she might have become suspicious."

Patricia was pretty certain Susie was telling the truth. "So, who sent you to my room, Susie?" she insisted. "Why are you acting as someone's stool pigeon?"

Susie tensed up and backed away to the door. "Look at me. I'm a chunky cookie. No guys ever take notice of me. So, when Foster asked to me to try and make you believe Lara's uncle was the killer…so what? Foster likes me."

"Foster…I should have known," Patricia whispered.

"I'll refuse to cooperate with the police. I'll tell the police you're the liar, not me. I'll claim you bullied me. I'll deny everything."

"You probably will," Patricia agreed. "Why? Because

you'll never understand when you're being used by a pretty face." Patricia shook her head. "Susie, all you have to do, honey, is have confidence in yourself—"

"I've tried," Susie exclaimed and then broke into tears. "Let me out of here. Right now."

Patricia shook her head again. Susie was through talking. She unlocked the door and let the young woman flee back to her own room.

"Okay, Foster, you're next on my list. But not now. Right now, I need some rest." Patricia closed her door, engaged the lock, and then walked back to the couch and plopped down. "Foster is Toby's stool pigeon. If Foster sent Susie to my room that means he took the order from Toby. Now I just need to figure out why Toby is here and how Karan plays into this nightmare."

Down the hall, unseen and unheard, Toby Ells pulled a sharp knife out from a gray suitcase. "In time," he hissed in a deadly voice. "In time...."

chapter four

Patricia heard a scream. Her eyes flew open. A heavy, thick, icy fog greeted her. It felt like a funeral sheet hanging down from a decayed stage filled with imprisoned nightmares. "Hello?" she called out in a confused, scared voice. "Is anyone there? I heard someone scream." Patricia's question was answered by a second scream...a scream belonging to a woman who seemed to be dying. "Hello? Please...where are you...I can't see...I...can try to help you...."

The icy fog formed into a white claw that tried to push Patricia back down onto the couch she had stood up from. She felt, rather than heard, a deadly voice hiss: "Get out of here or die." Patricia wanted to obey but something deep inside of her heart—a sense of... connection—forced her to move deeper into the fog. "Hello? Hello.... Where are you?"

The dying woman let out a third scream. "He's...killing me...help me!"

"How?" Patricia begged, pushing her way through the fog, struggling to move in the direction the woman's scream seemed to have come from. "Where are you? All I can see is white...help me to find you...please."

Patricia felt a hot breath burst out of the fog and strike her face. The breath smelled of strong whiskey and hate. "Get out of here or die!" a man's voice hissed at her, speaking to Patricia's heart rather than her ears. "This doesn't involve you."

"Please...he'll kill me...in the corner...beside the bed..." the woman cried out in an agonizing scream.

Patricia hurried through the fog. "I'm trying to find you...hold on," she begged. "I'm—" Patricia was interrupted when her outstretched arms struck a large bed. "I found the bed...hold on... keep talking to me."

"Get out of here!" the man hissed at Patricia again. "This doesn't involve you. If you don't leave you will die."

"Help me!" the woman screamed.

Patricia stared into the white, blinding fog. "I can't see...I'll work my way around the bed with my hands..."

"Get out or die!"

"No!" Patricia yelled. "Leave her alone...." Surprised at her own courage, Patricia began moving around the bed as quickly as possible. The fog formed into an angry mouth that began hissing at her. "I'm coming...hold on...hold on...."

"So be it," the man hissed at Patricia, and then a creepy feeling erupted, far creepier than what Patricia was already feeling...as if someone had suddenly clamped their hands down over the fog and wadded it up into a tight ball. Patricia felt her body turn to ice. She froze, unable to take a single step forward. "Have it your way," the man hissed again. "See for yourself."

To Patricia's horror the fog began to lift. The room she remembered being assigned to by Ben Grands began materializing. First the bed...then the walls...the floor...the couch...a window that wasn't boarded up. And then...slumped over in the far corner...a woman. A tall, vicious-looking man was standing over the woman holding a piece of rope in his hands. "The truth isn't what it appears," he growled at Patricia. "Some secrets need to remain buried." The man then ran to the window and threw his body through the glass.

Patricia managed to break the paralysis holding her captive and hurried to the window. To her shock she spotted the man stand up *off a rainy, muddy ground and begin to limp away into a dark storm. "But Ben said you killed yourself...you're supposed to be dead...Henry Graves is supposed to be dead...."*

Patricia jerked awake. For a few seconds she felt her mind still trapped at the broken window, staring down at a killer who had managed to survive a dangerous fall and escape into a horrible storm. The sound of someone knocking at her door slowly brought her mind out of the nightmare that had captured her.

"Ms. McKay? Ms. McKay...are you in there?" It was Ben Grands. "Ms. McKay?"

Feeling as if her mind had been pulled through a meat grinder, Patricia struggled to focus. Where was she? What was she lying on? Using her hands Patricia began to explore the old couch that had become her bed. "Oh...my back," she moaned. She slowly slid off the couch onto a pair of wobbly legs and looked around the very spooky, but lavish, room. "Oh...I was hoping all of this had been a nightmare."

"Ms. McKay? Ms. McKay?" Ben kept knocking.

"One...second." Patricia hobbled over to the door, disengaged the lock, and eased the door open. "Yes, Mr. Graves...Grands?"

A look of relief appeared on Ben's pale face. "Breakfast," he explained. "It's seven o'clock."

"Seven o'clock?" Patricia repeated in a weary voice. "I... must have fallen asleep."

"I haven't been able to sleep a single second," Ben confessed, still wearing the same suit from the night before. The poor man looked disheveled and plum worn out. "I can't quit thinking about my niece...that poor girl."

Patricia took a few seconds to wake her mind up before speaking. "Are the police still here?"

"Some young kid name Trent Richardson is downstairs on duty," Ben explained. "Chief Winchester left a few hours ago." Ben sighed. "Gary Horne will take over for Trent

Richardson tonight. That guy…he really thinks he's special."

"Arrogance suits him," Patricia agreed and then yawned. "I had the strangest dream," she told Ben and then shook her head as her eyes locked on to the older man. "Why did you assign me this room, Ben?" she asked. "Assigning someone to stay in a room where a murder occurred is kind of strange."

Ben glanced down the long, spooky hallway. "Mind if I step inside?"

"Be my guest." Patricia stepped away from the door and let Ben enter.

"The storm is worse now than it was last night," Ben said as he stepped into the room. "Trent Richardson had to arrive on a snowmobile. Radio said the storm has grown stronger and isn't supposed to weaken until tomorrow morning."

"Just dandy," Patricia sighed as her mouth began whining for a toothbrush. There was no time to brush her teeth, though. Maybe after breakfast…or lunch? Patricia was caught in the middle of a blizzard…and a murder. Her pearly white teeth would just have to suffer for a few hours. "Ben—"

"Let me explain," Ben pleaded as he studied the spooky room with curious eyes. "I haven't opened this room up since I arrived," he spoke in a sad voice. "I guess I didn't have the heart."

"The heart?"

Ben walked to the large bed and used a finger to scoop dust up off the blanket. "Last night, when I was telling you all about Henry Graves, I knew Lara was listening. I…told you what I wanted Lara to hear." Ben dusted his finger against his thumb and then turned to face Patricia. "My wife…well intentioned, of course, suggested Lara write a book on this manor. Melinda has a genuine caring heart to her and was always trying to help her niece."

Patricia heard regret hit Ben's voice. "Mr. Grands…

Graves…Ben, you didn't tell me the entire truth last night, did you?"

"No," Ben confessed. "How could I? Lara was listening. If Lara found out the truth…." Ben touched the bed again. "Not even Melinda knows the whole truth. Melinda thinks I'm in this for a few laughs in order to make a few pennies." Ben walked away from the bed and approached the couch. "I told Melinda my reasons for wanting to start the Dead and Breakfast. She has a good sense of humor and decided to play along. After all, we're not spring chickens anymore and we need a way to earn a living."

"When did your wife contact Lara?"

Ben stared down at the floor with weary eyes. "About two months ago," he answered as if he had a million pounds attached to his voice. He grew silent for a few moments. "Ms. McKay," he finally spoke, "I meant what I said last night. I do want to get the last laugh on Henry Graves. The curse did begin with him, but not in the way I implied."

Patricia forced her mind to wake up and really begin soaking in all the words Ben was speaking. "Oh?"

Ben reluctantly sat down on the green couch. "I'm not here to run a bed-and-breakfast…or as I call it, the Dead and Breakfast, for the rest of my life, Ms. McKay. As a matter of fact, I only intend…or intended…to call this cursed manor home for a short period of time." Ben touched the cushions attached to the green couch with weary hands. "It was Melinda's idea to allow you to come. When your boss contacted Melinda, she was thrilled. Of course, Melinda didn't know my real intentions."

"Which were?" Patricia dared to ask.

Ben shook his head. "Let me explain about this room first," he said.

"Sure," Patricia agreed in a polite voice. She walked over to the couch and sat down next to Ben. "I'm all ears."

Ben stared into Patricia's caring, honest eyes and sighed.

"You're well acquainted with murder, aren't you? Yes. I can see that truth hidden in your eyes."

For whatever reason Patricia's mind lurched back in time and ended up in Paris again. She saw herself sitting in a crummy motel room that was home to cranky rats and a very strange, mentally deranged woman...and then she herself fighting with a vicious killer. The spooky room she was sitting in now reminded Patricia of the shabby room in Paris...of the killer she had managed to defeat...of many things. "Paris certainly wasn't the city of romance."

"What?" Ben asked.

"Oh...nothing," Patricia answered and offered Ben a weak smile. "I was just thinking back to a time when I visited Paris and became involved in a very complicated murder case. Of course, Arizona was no walk in the park, either...and nearly being strangled to death in a corn maze wasn't exactly thrilling."

"Seems like you've had your share of—"

"Fighting with killers...yes." Patricia nodded and gently patted Ben's arm. "I've had my share of nightmares, Ben. Now, tell me why you assigned to me room eight."

Ben shifted his eyes to the large bed. "I lied," he confessed. "I lied because Lara was listening and she couldn't know the truth. Lara believes we're related to Henry Graves."

"But...you're not?" Patricia asked.

Ben shook his head. "Ms. McKay, I'm related to Veronica Drakes. That's why I didn't have the heart to enter this room."

"Then why—"

"Assign you to this room?" Ben asked. Patricia nodded. "I had no other choice. When the other guests began mysteriously showing up, I began to have a bad feeling. After all, Ms. McKay, who shows up at an unknown bed-and-breakfast in the middle of a snowstorm? One person maybe, someone out traveling and wanting to get off the roads. But multiple guests? It was strange. And on top of that I had to keep Lara snooping around in here. And I also had to make it seem like I was dumb to the truth myself. I told Lara, in front of the guests, that room eight was reserved for you—the travel writer—whenever you arrived. I added a lot of shine to my statement too, showing fake excitement and claiming you were going to put this cursed place on the map. Of course, Lara had to chime in and claim she was going to write a bestselling novel." Ben sighed. "Lara...I still can't believe that poor girl is dead."

Patricia stared at Ben and then took a minute to put his words together inside of her mind. *Ben lied to me because Lara was listening in...I can accept that. Ben also assigned me to this room to keep the other guests out. Okay. I can accept that. But why hasn't Ben entered this room until now? What has kept him out? It's obvious he's looking for something...at least that's how it seems.*

"Ben, I think Lara was killed because someone didn't want her writing a book about this manor."

"Yes, I believe that's the reason my niece was killed too," Ben said with sad eyes. "Lara knew I was lying to her, Ms. McKay. She knew the facts—but I kept insisting that she was wrong. That's why I told you I was related to Griffin North last night, because Lara was listening. Maybe...if she heard me talking to you...telling you the same facts I insisted were true...she might have relented and believed me."

"Lara knew the truth about Veronica Drakes?"

"Yes," Ben confessed in a tormented voice. "How? I don't know. No one knew the truth except my mother—and my mother told me all the details on her death bed." Ben made a painful face. "I was never close to my mother...and I suppose she wanted to clear her conscience and somehow make retribution. I don't know. All I do know is that she left me this manor with one request attached to the deed."

"Request?"

Ben allowed silence to fall before answering Patricia's

question. He scanned the spooky room and then sighed. "Burn the manor down."

"I...see," Patricia answered in a careful tone. "But not before...finding some type of hidden treasure?"

Ben glanced over at Patricia. "You're a very smart young lady, Ms. McKay."

"My smart mind gets me into lots and lots of trouble," Patricia confessed. She stood up and walked over to the boarded-up window. "Mr. Grands...Ben...Henry Graves didn't kill Veronica Drakes, did he?"

Ben felt his face turn white as a sheet. "No," he answered in a low whisper.

"Veronica Drakes was murdered by her husband, wasn't she?"

Ben looked as if someone had punched him in the gut. "Yes."

Patricia glanced toward the corner that once held the body of a delicate woman. "The question is...why?" she asked. "You stated Henry Graves married Veronica Drakes, but that's not true."

"That's the official story."

"But—"

"Veronica Drakes was not married to Henry Graves," Ben confirmed. "Henry Graves was the...scapegoat. Once Veronica Drakes's real husband found out Henry's true mission—and that his wife was assisting Henry because she sympathized with the South—he altered history along with all the true facts. But history has a way of correcting itself."

Patricia continued to stare at the corner that once held the body of Veronica Drakes. "Henry Graves didn't die, did he?" she asked as her mind returned back to her nightmare. "No. Henry Graves didn't die. He escaped."

Ben didn't respond.

"Ben, I understand that you're a comedian—"

"A comedian who worked as a ventriloquist," Ben pointed out in a tired voice. "The head you saw attached to the stick I was holding used to belong to a puppet named Charles. Charles was one of my greatest acts…now he's just a head."

Patricia felt sorry for Ben. In her eyes—and maybe the eyes of everyone who once knew and respected Ben—the guy was a sad and lonely washed-out comedian. "What I meant to say, Ben, was that I understand why you used your retirement as a comedian to disguise the real reason you purchased this manor."

"Well, Ms. McKay, as I stated earlier, my mother left me this cursed manor…I didn't exactly purchase it. All I did was pay a few back taxes. The county was getting ready to grab this land and this manor away from my mother before she died," Ben explained. "But in order to keep everything in the green…yes, I did make my arrival appear to be an official real estate purchase. I had a very dire secret to protect."

Patricia stared at Ben. "How did you manage—"

"To make the official papers reflect more than a few paid off back taxes?" Ben asked. Patricia nodded. "Melinda was away seeing her sick sister again…for the millionth time… while I was sitting with my mother. After I learned the truth, I paid off the needed back taxes but then sold the land and manor to a friend of mine. I gave him the money to buy the land and the manor, and then I simply bought the land and manor right back, using a…well, less than honest real estate company to help me. Why? Because I had a secret to protect, but more importantly, I had my wife to protect. If anyone found out that I knew the truth…." Ben shook his head. "You're a smart woman, Ms. McKay. You can figure out the rest."

"I can," Patricia assured Ben. She approached the couch and sat down. "Ben, before I ask a very obvious question, I want to ask you about the guests, beginning with Toby Ells."

"The archaeology major."

"Yes," Patricia confirmed, her eyes feeling heavy. Oh, how she yearned for a warm, soft bed and a full twelve hours of solid sleep. And to make matters worse, her stomach was beginning to grumble. "Could it be that Toby Ells is searching for what you're looking for?"

"I have considered that," Ben confessed.

Patricia glanced at the door. Was anyone standing out in the hallway listening? No. Ben had assured her Officer Trent had ordered everyone to remain downstairs once they left their room. But still...were there other means of listening, like through a hidden passageway? Patricia felt it was possible, and that's why she had yet to ask Ben what treasure he was seeking out.

"When did Toby Ells show up, Ben?"

"Yesterday around noon," Ben explained. "About half an hour later, Foster showed up, and about, oh, around two o'clock, that strange woman Karan showed up claiming she had arrived to conduct an interview on the manor after a friend told her about it. Lara and her friend Susie were already here."

Patricia scratched at her nose, fighting the urge to sneeze. Boy, was the room dusty...and was she ever hungry too. Working on an empty stomach wasn't very fun. *I'm going to punch Edna in the nose when I get home.* "Oh...I love the game of *Clue. You must simply drive to Ohio and write about this new, fantastic bed-and-breakfast...and while you're at it...figure out a real-life murder."*

"Edna...."

"Edna?" Ben asked.

Patricia sighed. "My boss. I was just thinking that when I get home, I might slug her for sending me here." Patricia rolled her eyes. "First Edna wanted me to believe she was excited about the idea of a spooky bed-and-breakfast, and then she confessed she wanted me to come here because her competition had managed to land a job writing about a series of murder mystery bed-and-breakfasts that are opening in Oregon—"

"I heard about those."

Patricia scratched at her nose again. "Seems like everyone has," she complained. "However, it seems like your bed-and-breakfast—well, this manor isn't exactly a bed-and-breakfast —is the real deal. We have a real-life game of Clue to play." Patricia looked down at Ben. "If Lara hadn't been murdered, you would have let me play my part, right?"

"Ms. McKay, my wife wanted you to travel to Ohio, not me," Ben explained. "In order to protect my secret, I had to play along. You were asked to come here to write out a murder mystery game script and then write a fun article on the place. I had to use that to my advantage." Ben stood up and stretched his back. "Lara was already causing me problems and when the other guests suddenly showed up, I knew something was off. But I couldn't let on I knew. Yesterday just became a big mess."

"You sure didn't seem upset when I arrived. As a matter of fact, you were clowning around with your wooden dummy."

"Ever hear of putting on a brave face?" Ben asked. He rubbed his lower back. "I had to keep my stage face on or else. And now that Lara...bless her heart...now that she's dead, you can understand why."

Patricia understood. "Ben, do you think Toby Ells is the killer?"

"Yes," Ben answered in a clear and honest voice that hid no hint of doubt. "I don't know how he killed Lara, but he did. I wanted to tell Chief Winchester my thoughts but Charles, my wooden dummy, has more brains than that man. Besides, if I confessed my thoughts, I might have turned myself into...a target." Ben locked eyes with Patricia. "Right now, I don't know what to do except keep my stage face on and keep acting like a grief-stricken uncle. Acting like a grief-stricken uncle is the easy part. My stage face…not so much."

Patricia began walking around the room. She wanted to ask more questions but it was clear Ben's battery was growing weaker and weaker. The man's eyes were bloodshot and filled with fatigue. Patricia feared if she kept pressing Ben, his mind might collapse. The man was under an incredible amount of stress. "I think I'll go downstairs and get some coffee and maybe a donut or two."

"I'll go with you." Ben glanced around the spooky room and then looked back at Patricia. He watched as Patricia grabbed her purse and room key. "Ready?"

"Wish I could brush my teeth…but that can wait. Let's go." Patricia walked Ben to the door, glanced back at the room, sighed, and then made her way out into the long hallway. As she did, she spotted Toby entering his room. "I thought you said all the guests were downstairs," she said to Ben.

"All the guests are supposed to be downstairs," Ben confirmed in a low whisper. "Stay here."

"Ben—"

"Stay here," Ben ordered and then marched up to closed brown door and knocked on it. "Mr. Ells, the guests are supposed to be downstairs."

Toby yanked the door open and glared at Ben. "I spilled coffee on my jacket. Officer Trent gave me permission to change," he snarled. "I'll be back downstairs in a few minutes." With those words Toby slammed the door shut.

Ben turned and looked at Patricia. Patricia hurried to Ben, took his hand, and walked him down the hallway. "Let's join the rest of the guests, okay. It'll be safer that way. Whatever Toby may or may not be up to, if we try to interfere, he might turn hostile," she whispered in a low voice. "If all the guests are downstairs and accounted for, at least we know he won't be able to harm anyone."

Ben didn't want to agree with Patricia's suggestion. He wanted to turn around and order Toby to go back downstairs. However, fatigue, stress, and fear overcame his will to stand strong. Lara was dead and Ben didn't want to join his niece. He had his wife to consider. "All right, we'll go down to the kitchen."

"Good," Patricia whispered, still holding on to Ben. "Lead the way."

Ben nodded and led Patricia down the creaky steps. Once downstairs, he walked down a long hallway that stood behind the main staircase and took Patricia into a large kitchen that was filled with shadows and gloom. Although already old and creepy, the room didn't need Ben's help in adding an extra layer of spookiness. The only bright spot Patricia found—if there was a bright spot—was the smell of warm coffee that was dancing in the kitchen air.

"I see everyone is present…except for Mr. Ells," Ben stated, walking into the kitchen with Patricia.

Patricia spotted Foster standing with Susie next to a worn wooden counter. Karan was sitting at a gloomy round table that was covered with some type of cloth that made Patricia think of a funeral sheet. Some skinny kid wearing a badge was leaning against the back door drinking a cup of coffee; he didn't look a day older than sixteen.

"Good morning, everyone," Patricia said and yawned. "I see no one else has changed into fresh clothes, either." Patricia motioned down at her dress. "Looks like we all slept uneasy."

Karan lifted her head and eyed Patricia with sour eyes but didn't say a word. Foster spoke instead. "You sure took your time getting downstairs for breakfast," he stated and then looked at Ben. "How long does it take to tell someone coffee and donuts are waiting in the kitchen?"

"What does it matter to you?" Ben snapped back. "Ms. McKay, coffee and donuts are on the counter. Help yourself."

Susie eyed Patricia with worried eyes. Patricia pretended

not to notice as she approached the counter, located a brown coffee mug, and poured herself a hot cup of coffee that she assumed wasn't poisoned. Officer Trent was present in the kitchen and Patricia knew the killer wouldn't try to make a drastic move with a law enforcement officer present—even if the officer was a kid with pimples who would most likely try to stop the killer from poisoning the coffee, which in turn might create a dead cop. Cops were connected to a grid—kill one cop and millions came running. The killer, Patricia told herself as she filled her cup, most likely didn't want the manor crawling with the state patrol and federal agents. Best to keep the situation nice and quiet and under control.

Coffee is safe, Patricia assured her sleepy mind as she grabbed a plain donut out of a brown and white donut box. "Boy, what a night. I'm so tired I can barely think straight."

Ben looked at Patricia with curious eyes. She wasn't acting like she had upstairs while speaking with him alone. "We're all tired."

"I guess so," Patricia agreed and said a quick prayer of thanks for the coffee and donuts. Thanking God through Jesus for any and all food was very important to Patricia. "I guess my boss won't be too happy that this story bombed out," she continued. "I was supposed to write a murder mystery game script and then a fun little article. But that isn't going to happen now."

"A woman is dead," Foster pointed out, taken aback by Patricia's sudden change. She wasn't acting like a clever Nancy Drew as she had the night before.

"Yeah, I know." Patricia nodded and then took a sip of coffee. "Wow...strong!" she exclaimed. "Boy, I'm going to be standing on my head later. Oh well, beats being dead...no offense."

"No offense?" Susie asked with an offended glare. "Lara is dead—"

"I know Lara is dead," Patricia complained and rolled her

eyes. "For crying out loud, I saw her body…I saw the knife, but what do you want me to do about it? I can't bring her back, can I?" Patricia set her coffee down and pointed her donut at Susie. "I tried to help last night, but now I have my career to worry about. My boss isn't going to be happy and I can't afford to lose my job."

Foster glared at Susie, who looked thoroughly confused. "She wasn't acting like this earlier," Susie whispered under her breath.

Ah, so Susie did tell Foster about our little talk, Patricia thought. "Look, people, I'm sorry Lara was killed, but I'm sure the killer is long gone by now. I'm pretty sure I'm right when I say the killer escaped into the storm and took the first exit out of town…so let's just all take a deep breath, okay." Patricia looked at Officer Trent. "Is it wrong for a gal to be worried about her career?"

"Uh…guess not?" Trent answered in a confused voice. Patricia sure was beautiful. Pretty girls made Trent nervous. "I mean…you had a job to do, right?"

"Right," Patricia stated and hurried to take a bite of donut. "So, look, don't anyone start breathing down my neck because I'm worried about my career."

"Who is breathing down your neck?" Karan's sour voice caught Patricia off guard. Patricia looked over at Karan and saw the woman staring up at her with venomous eyes. "We all have our own problems, so stop complaining about yours," Karan sniped.

"You're one to talk," Patricia huffed. "All you do is go around and look at places that are so-called spooky attractions. It's not like you have a professional career to worry about like me."

"Hey, my work is very professional," Karan snapped at Patricia. "I'm an established paranormal investigator—"

"Give me a break," Patricia said, rolling her eyes. She gobbled down the rest of her donut and then looked at Karan again. "But then again…maybe not? I mean, a woman is dead and there you sit. Maybe you had some inside information, huh?"

Karan glared at Patricia with fire in her eyes. "Are you suggesting I was somehow involved with the murder?"

"All I'm saying is that you showed up at the right time," Patricia responded. "But hey, what's it to me? The cops are on the job, right?" Patricia tossed a fake flirty smile at Trent. "I have my career to worry about…and some bad coffee to get down." Patricia picked her coffee back up and took a sip. "Wow…strong."

Foster glared at Susie. Susie winced. Karan glanced at Foster with a quick eye but didn't say a word. Toby walked into the kitchen wearing a large frown. He marched to the kitchen table and sat down. "Coffee," he barked at Foster. Foster nodded.

Well, at least we're all present and accounted for, Patricia thought, taking another sip of coffee. *Now the fun really begins.*

Outside the snowstorm continued to scream and howl.

chapter five

T oby glanced at Patricia with eyes that could kill. His attention swiftly moved to Ben and traveled to Susie. Susie was nibbling on a donut like a nervous mouse while Foster worked on a cup of coffee. Patricia noticed that Toby didn't look at Karan. Why? Were Toby and Karan somehow connected? And why did Toby walk his eyes past Trent without any concern? Did Toby consider Trent to be more of a nuisance than a threat? *Most likely*, Patricia thought, taking a sip of coffee. Toby was a large man—powerful and deadly. A little squirt like Trent was of no concern to a man like Toby. Still, Trent was a cop, and cops were connected to a network. Patricia seriously doubted Toby wanted to attract more flies to the honey bowl.

"Well, this storm sure put a damper on today, didn't it?" Patricia asked in an annoyed tone, deciding to latch on to the part of a dimwit. While it was true she had showed her true detective skills the night before, Patricia hoped her change of attitude would be accepted. After all, only Ben and Foster had really seen her detective skills in play. Perhaps Toby and Karan, if they were informed by Foster that a Nancy Drew–type character was present, would assume the information that was given to them was…unstable. "Boy, is my boss mad too."

"Enough with your boss already," Karan snapped at Patricia. She locked her eyes on Trent. "When can we leave the kitchen?"

"When Chief Winchester calls me," Trent replied, eating a chocolate-covered donut that likely would cause more pimples. "Chief Winchester told me to keep all the guests in the kitchen, so, uh, just relax and have a donut."

"I don't eat processed foods," Karan informed Trent, adding an extra layer of ice to her voice. "I want to continue with my work."

"Work?" Patricia asked, pretending to sound confused.

"I'm a paranormal investigator, remember?" Karan snapped. "I didn't drive all this way to be sidelined by an unfortunate murder." Karan looked at Ben. "If allowed, I can distinguish the truth about this manor from fiction and help you establish a credible reputation. When I arrived you put up resistance, but as I stated, if you would just allow me to examine this manor and conduct an investigation—"

"No," Ben answered in a stern tone. "My answer now is the same as yesterday."

Ben didn't tell me he was having trouble with Karan, Patricia thought as a cloud of worry entered her mind. *Karan seems very adamant to continue her work. Toby doesn't seem very supportive, either.* Toby had his head turned and was looking at Karan with harsh eyes. *What is the deal between those two? Maybe it's time to find out.*

"Speaking of work, maybe I can salvage my job," Patricia stated in a hopeful voice. "Mr. Ells, you're a college professor, right? You teach archaeology? I'm sure you must have some interesting stories to tell about your travels."

Toby rotated his eyes back to Patricia. "I don't give interviews."

Wow, this guy is a real sour rock. Can't imagine him being a teacher. "Sure, okay," Patricia answered in a voice tainted with indifference. "Whatever floats your boat. Just need a story." Patricia decided to add some heat to her statement while remaining indifferent. "Maybe I'll just write about this manor. I mean, it's not like this place has no history. Sure, my boss is upset that my original piece fell flat, but maybe I can salvage enough to make an interesting little puzzle for my readers." Patricia looked at Ben. "Do you know the magazine I work for has over twenty million readers?" Patricia had no idea how many people actually read the travel magazine, but she wanted to shake Toby up.

"That many readers would certainly be good for the Dead and Breakfast," Ben said, supporting Patricia. Whatever scheme Patricia was creating…whatever trap the clever woman was throwing down onto the floor…Ben was all for it. "The more readers the better."

Patricia agreed. "And you know what, Mr. Graves?" she added in a quick voice, throwing on her thoughtful face. "I can use some elbow grease and really dig into the history of this old place. I mean, why not? So, what if my original piece fell flat? A good writer knows how to salvage a story. I'll write a history piece instead of a humor piece. I know I'm known for my humor, and maybe writing a history piece won't exactly have my readers rolling on the floor, but hey, I have my career to save."

Patricia glanced at Toby. The man was staring at her with steaming eyes. Patricia knew it was time to punch the man in the nose. "And you know what, after all the facts Lara told me before she was…uh…unfortunately killed…I think I might have enough ingredients to write a good piece—after I do a bit of research on my own, of course, to make sure the facts Lara told me are not fictional."

Toby balled his hands into two furious fists. "Perhaps I can give you an interview after all," he informed Patricia, speaking through gritted teeth. "I'm certain my interview would be far more compelling."

Bingo! "Uh, let me think about it, okay, Mr. Ells. I'll call my boss and run everything past her. Old Edna isn't one to have her hands holding only air, you know. She'll insist I write something," Patricia explained in a casual tone. *If that guy gets me alone, I'm a goner,* Patricia warned herself. *It's time to play this game with a very, very clever mind.*

"Of...course," Toby replied in a sour voice. "I'll wait for your answer. I won't be leaving anytime soon."

"Oh?" Patricia asked. "Even after the murder?"

"I'm on vacation," Toby answered.

"You sure picked a strange hotel...bed-and-breakfast...whatever you want to call this creepy place," Patricia told Toby. "Next time stay at a nice hotel or with a family member."

"I'll remember that." Toby snatched up a cup of coffee and took a sip. "I'll also remember to check the weather."

"That would help." Patricia tittered and then acted as she if were more interested in the donut she was eating. "Ben, these donuts are a tad stale."

"Sorry," Ben apologized.

"What's with you?" Susie barked at Patricia, unable to hold back her confusion and anger any longer. "You're not acting like you were earlier. You're acting like a nitwit. Why?"

"A nitwit?" Patricia asked, pretending to sound offended. "So, I'm a nitwit for wanting to salvage my career? Figures someone from California would say such a thing."

"What's that supposed to mean?" Susie snapped.

"California—duh!" Patricia snapped back. "California isn't exactly the brightest state on the map."

"Hey, I resent that. California has a lot of intelligent people—"

"And you're not one of them!" Patricia attacked Susie in an insulting voice, hoping to deliberately create a fight. "I'm pretty sure the few measly brain cells floating around in your empty skull are begging to be put down."

"I…how dare you!" Susie yelled at Patricia. "I happen to be working on my bachelor's degree—"

"Let me guess…at some liberal arts college?" Patricia rolled her eyes to add insult to injury—or was it injury to insult? She didn't care.

"I…well, so what if I am?" Susie fumbled over her words and then looked down at her hands and grew silent.

"Leave her alone," Foster barked at Patricia. "Who are you to judge? It's not like you're a doctor. You're a travel writer. Everyone get up and do a happy dance."

Patricia shrugged. "My degree in journalism isn't a piece of gold. A gal has to take whatever writing gigs are thrown her way."

"Enough," Trent ordered, trying to sound tough. "Look, I know you're all upset, but biting at each other's neck isn't going to solve your problems." Trent had heard a famous cop say the line he spoke on a television show. Yeah, using a lame line was…lame, but Trent wasn't exactly Perry Mason.

"He's right," Karan said. "Lara Braceton is dead. Right now, I think we all need to calm down and focus on why we all came here."

"And why did you come here?" Patricia asked Foster, throwing an "and just who are you to talk" voice at him. "What do you do for a living, huh?"

Foster glanced at Toby, who shook his head. "I…uh, work as a teacher's assistant," Foster announced in a quick, low tone.

You work as Toby's servant, Patricia thought to herself, growing sick of acting like a dimwitted moron. *I think I have enough information now to work on for a while. I need to call Brian and see what he's doing.*

"Officer, I need to use the lady's room. The coffee…well, coffee makes me have to really go."

"There's a bathroom through that door," Ben explained, pointing to a door that was sitting close to the pantry door. "You'll find a short hallway. Bathroom is at the end."

"I don't know," Trent objected. "Chief Winchester told me to keep everyone in the kitchen."

"Don't worry," Ben assured Trent. "The hallway has no windows and neither does the bathroom. There's really no way out."

"Please," Patricia begged Trent. "I've gotta go."

Trent nervously bit down on his lip. "Oh, let her go," Karan complained. "We're entitled to bathroom breaks."

Trent hesitated and then nodded.

"Thanks!" Patricia grabbed her purse and hurried away. A few minutes later she found herself locked in a creepy old bathroom that was lit by a bare bulb hanging on a wire that was dripping from a decaying ceiling. "Just like in the movies," she whispered, staring at a broken mirror attached to a rusted medicine cabinet. A toilet that appeared to have sprouted a new form of bacteria sat next to a rust-stained bathroom sink. Patricia wanted to vomit but there was no time. She had to call Brian. "Be up."

Brian picked up on the third ring. "Nothing yet," he announced without saying hello. "I've just gotten into my office. I've spent the last hour fussing with the mayor...so give me some time to work on the names you gave me."

Patricia heard clear irritation in Brian's voice that made her heart drop. So much for a warm and welcoming hello. "If you're fussing with the mayor—"

"The governor wasn't happy that I made my report public," Brian explained, crashing down into his desk chair like a bag of hard potatoes. "I let the local newspaper publish my report—on purpose. I knew if I sent it off without a few public hands on it the jerks down in Atlanta would change it to match their agenda. Almost got canned, but the chief stood by me and threatened to resign if the mayor insisted on firing me."

"Sounds like you had a very hard morning. I'm sorry."

"Don't be," Brian told Patricia, setting down a brown cup of coffee on his desk. "I released the report yesterday. I guess I should have told you, but I wanted to wait to see how the frog boiled in the pot." Brian shook his head. "The jerks down in Atlanta do not like being proven wrong. Next time they'll think twice about breathing down my neck. I'm just glad this mess is behind me. Now maybe I can focus on some real police work...like writing a few parking tickets."

"Sounds like our little mountain town isn't as peaceful as the brochures make out," Patricia told Brian in a tired voice. "Trouble is everywhere."

"Trouble can find a sleeping ladybug hiding under an autumn leaf," Brian agreed and then decided to focus on Patricia's case. "How are things at the Dead and Breakfast?" he asked.

"Snowy, stormy, and ugly," Patricia said, doing her best to stand in one place without touching anything. *I'll have to burn my shoes later.* "I'm not exactly certain yet, but I think Toby Ells might be the killer."

"But?" Brian asked, reading a curious tone in Patricia's voice.

Patricia began nibbling on her lip. "Brian, listen," she whispered and quickly told Brian about the talk she had with Ben earlier in the morning. "Ben is searching for a treasure, and Toby, Karan, maybe even Susie, they must know about the treasure. Why else would they be here?"

"What about the Foster guy?" Brian asked.

"I'm pretty sure Foster isn't a killer. He's Toby's errand dog," Patricia said in a low whisper. "That doesn't mean the guy isn't dangerous, though."

"It doesn't take a veteran cop to see that everyone who

showed up at the Dead and Breakfast did so with a hidden agenda," Brian said in a careful voice.

"Any cop with a brain cell, that is," Patricia told Brian. "The cops in Whispering Hills are clueless…and to make matters worse, they're trying to operate in a snowstorm and half the force is out sick." Patricia saw Toby's dangerous face appear in her worried mind. "Brian, Toby Ells strikes me as the type of guy who isn't afraid or too concerned about a few empty-headed cops. My gut is telling me that Toby Ells isn't planning on leaving this creepy manor empty-handed."

"Patricia, I can try and drive up—"

"Not in this storm," Patricia sighed. "Brian, I'm snowed in…and so is everyone else. For now…the game of Clue just has to play itself out." Patricia grew silent for a moment as her eyes explored the bathroom. *If I see a rat I'll scream.* "Brian, the more I think about it, the more I think it may—and I say this very carefully—it may be possible that Toby Ells isn't the killer after all."

"Oh? Who else is in the spotlight?" Brian asked.

Patricia closed her eyes and saw a face appear. "I better not say…just yet," she whispered. "If I'm wrong, I'll never forgive myself."

Brian understood. Patricia was the type of woman who methodically worked her way through a case by utilizing her critical thinking skills—no fancy forensic gadgets, no fancy computers, no team of experts working on her side. Just Patricia and her mind, a strange but beautiful mind that always kept Brian on his toes.

"Okay…I tell you what," Brian said. "I'll get to work and call you when I find something that may be of some help to you."

"Okay, honey," Patricia spoke in a soft voice. "I'll be waiting for your call…and thank you." Patricia put the cell phone she was holding back into her purse. "Well," she spoke aloud, looking around the bathroom, "the game of Clue certainly is fun when the murder victim is just a game character. In real life, it stinks." With those words Patricia left the bathroom and made her way back to the parlor and prepared for a very long and dangerous day.

"Yes, Chief." Trent shoved his gray cell phone into the pocket of his police coat and made a happy face. "Gary will be here soon," he announced.

"How wonderful," Karan replied in a very ugly, sarcastic voice. "We've been trapped in this dreadful room for most of the day and now we get to remain here for the rest of the night under the careful watch of Dr. Doolittle."

Patricia had to admit that being forced to remain in the front room of the manor all day wasn't exactly thrilling. But to her relief everyone present seemed to have drifted off into their own world of silence. Not a single incident occurred. Toby, Karan, and Susie focused on reading while Foster played solitaire on his cell phone. Ben finally crashed in a drab sitting chair and ended up snoring most of the day away while Trent stood guard close to the front door yapping away to his girlfriend. The storm outside had not abated, and, as Trent announced, it was now trapped in a slow-moving system that was now stalled over the area.

Trent thought Karan was pretty—even if the woman was past forty...or fifty, he wasn't sure. Pretty or not, he wasn't going to stand by and let her insult his friend. "Gary is a good cop, lady. Show some respect, huh?"

Karan rolled her eyes. "I'm trapped in Green Acres."

"Green Acres?" Trent looked confused.

"The old television show...remember?" Susie said, lowering her book. "*Green Acres* was an old TV show—"

"Never heard of it," Trent cut Susie off. "I try to watch

modern shows," he explained, trying to sound hip and modern. "The old stuff is too dusty for me."

"Whatever," Susie snapped and went back to her book. And why not? Foster was ignoring her. As far as Susie was concerned, Foster's silence toward her was just fine. She was through with trying to impress jerks. "I'll become a nun," she whispered under her breath and then shot Foster a sour eye. Foster ignored the look.

Patricia checked her watch. It was almost seven o'clock. "Will Officer Horne be arriving by snowmobile?" she asked Trent.

"How else could he get here?" Trent asked back. "No way a car or even an SUV is getting up these country roads."

Patricia nodded. If Toby was the killer he might strike during the night and escape on Gary's snowmobile. However, Patricia wasn't so certain Toby would strike. It was clear that Ben was after a hidden treasure and that Toby and Karan were aware of the treasure. Would Toby kill again and escape into the snowstorm without the treasure? Patricia doubted it. But what if Toby wasn't the killer? What if Karan was the killer? *Karan isn't the killer. Foster isn't the killer. Ben isn't the killer.* Patricia walked her eyes over to Susie. Susie glanced up from her book, looked at Patricia, grimaced, and then went back to reading.

"Ben, how about some coffee?" Patricia said.

"No one leaves this room. Chief's orders," Trent told Patricia in a quick, stern tone.

Ben stood up from the chair he had been sleeping in all day, stretched his sore back, and then rubbed his chin. "Officer, we haven't had any dinner. For lunch everyone was served a measly sandwich. Now, you can arrest me if you want, but I'm going to the kitchen and prepare a meal and make a pot of coffee."

"We do need to eat," Karan insisted. She stood up from a

red couch and rubbed the small of her back. "Mr. Graves, I can help you in the kitchen if you would like."

"No, I can manage," Ben assured Karan, attempting to sound very polite. "My wife has taught this old lazy dog a few tricks, and one of those tricks is how to use a pot and pan while she's away."

"Mr. Graves—" Trent began to object.

"We're not in jail. And even prisoners get to eat. You can't starve us," Ben warned Trent and then bravely walked out of the front room.

Trent looked upset and followed after Ben. "Everyone stay in this room and that's an order. I'll watch Mr. Graves," he called back over his shoulder.

"Stay in this room...not likely. I'm going to help Mr. Graves in the kitchen whether he likes it or not," Karan growled and stormed out of the front room.

Patricia glanced at Toby, Foster, and Susie. All three of her enemies were now staring at Karan as the woman marched away.

"I need to use the bathroom...really bad," Foster finally spoke. "I'll go use the one in the kitchen. Toby nodded. Foster quickly hurried away.

"Well, if everyone is going to the kitchen I might as well go too," Susie announced. "I'm very hungry."

Patricia watched Susie leave the front room, leaving her alone with Toby. Toby slowly shifted his eyes over to Patricia. "You think I killed that girl, don't you? Sure you do," he said in a low, dangerous tone.

Patricia, to Toby's shock, shook her head no. "I did at first," she confessed, standing near a cobblestone fireplace holding a low fire. "You're a dangerous man, Mr. Ells."

"Only to my enemies...and to those who stand in my way," Toby assured Patricia in a tone that made it clear that no one stood in his way.

Patricia studied Toby's stone face. "What are you after, Mr. Ells?"

"It's nice to see that you've stopped playing your silly game," Toby told Patricia. He calmly walked over to a green sitting chair and sat down. "You didn't fool me this morning. You did, however, fool Foster, Karan, and Susie. I'm impressed."

"What are you after Mr. Ells?" Patricia pressed, ignoring Toby's statement. You're an archaeology major. You certainly didn't drive to Ohio to spend the night in this cursed manor. You're obviously searching for something...and so is Karan."

Toby folded his hands together and glared at Patricia. "What has Mr. Grands told you?"

Patricia shook her head. "What Mr. Grands and I have talked about is secret...for now."

"Secrets get people killed around here."

"I know," Patricia agreed and then dared to point a brave finger at Toby. "But you're not a killer. I thought you were, at first—"

"What changed your mind?"

Patricia slowly clasped her hands behind her back while making sure her purse was perched safely on the wooden mantel that was just an arm's reach away. "To begin with, you came downstairs with Susie and Karan last night. You had no snow on your shoes. Of course, that didn't mean you couldn't have sneaked back inside after killing Lara, changed your shoes, and whatnot. There are many possibilities."

"But you have concluded that I'm not the killer."

"Mr. Ells, you are after something...a hidden treasure of some sort." Patricia grew silent for a moment and listened to the storm howl and scream outside. "Why would you risk losing the opportunity to acquire what you are searching for? Killing Lara would have meant the cops would have shut this manor down, and if it wasn't for this storm, I'm certain Chief

Winchester would have hauled everyone down to the local jail."

"Very perceptive."

"It took me most of the day to realize that you are not the killer, Mr. Ells," Patricia confessed. "When you announced this morning that you weren't leaving this manor anytime soon, I couldn't help but feel that you truly meant your words."

"I did," Toby assured Patricia. "You are a very intelligent woman, Ms. McKay. I'm impressed."

"I don't need compliments. I need facts," Patricia told Toby. "What are you searching for, Mr. Ells? I assure you that whatever treasure you are after is of no concern to me. All I want is the truth."

"In order to publish the truth in your travel magazine?"

"No," Patricia promised. "My story is now dead. If my boss presses me to write a piece on this manor...this awful place...I'll scratch up a quick humor piece just to please her eyes."

Toby studied Patricia. To his relief the woman was speaking the absolute truth. "Very well, Ms. McKay. I will confess the reason for my...visit," he announced in a low, gruff voice, and then focused his deadly eyes on the fireplace. "I drove to Whispering Hills to find my brother. My brother is the hidden treasure that I was searching for."

"Your brother...." Patricia stared at Toby in confusion. However, the cloud of confusion that dropped over her mind quickly faded. "Ben Grands?"

Toby nodded. "Last year the private detective agency I have been partnering with to find my brother located some very interesting information."

"I'm all ears."

"I assumed you would be." Toby kept his eyes on the fireplace. "My search initially was not for a brother. I was searching for...my mother, Ms. McKay. Last year it was discovered that my mother had died. However, I was informed that I had a brother." Toby closed his eyes. "All of my life I've walked through history, searching for truth, while denying my own life the very truth I needed the most. At the age of forty-eight I finally decided to seek out the mother who deserted me at birth. I had very little information to work from…just a name."

"Mr. Ells—"

"You want to know why I appear to be so deadly?" Toby cut Patricia off.

"Yes."

Toby eyes slowly opened—like the eyes of a dead man opening from a long sleep. "Ms. McKay, my field is archaeology; however, I also majored in crime. I'm currently employed by a very well-known and very dangerous mafia family in Los Angeles—but not by choice."

"I don't understand."

"Blackmail, plain and simple," Toby said in a low growl. "All my life I have been forced to become a monster or risk spending the rest of my life behind bars for a mistake I made when I was nineteen years old."

"What happened when you were nineteen?" Patricia asked in a careful tone. Toby was opening up his thoughts and Patricia didn't want to push the man into a corner.

"I killed a man," Toby spoke in a low voice. "It was self-defense, but who would have believed me? I was a young college kid. Green behind the ears." In Toby's mind he saw a young kid run down a man aiming a gun at him. "It was either kill or be killed. I had no choice."

"Someone saw the killing?"

"I killed the son of a very dangerous mafia boss," Toby confessed. "The enemy of this man saw me do it and forced me to work for him—or risk going to prison for murder, or even worse, risk being hunted down and killed."

"So, you agreed?"

"Yes." Toby nodded. "I agreed. In return I was allowed to finish my education while I was assigned to start smuggling drugs into the country. My work in archaeology was the perfect smuggling tunnel." Toby looked up at Patricia. "Ever work for a mafia family, Ms. McKay? Sometimes you have to kill in order to stay alive."

"I'm sure you do," Patricia said.

Toby lowered his gaze. "It's time for me to escape, Ms. McKay. I decided to find my brother and begin a new life... with what life I have left to live. I left Los Angeles without permission. I can never return. If I do, I'm a dead man."

"How does Foster play into this?" Patricia asked, gently pressing forward.

Toby grew silent for a moment. When he spoke, his voice entered the air defeated rather than angry. "Foster is my...son."

Toby's announcement didn't shock Patricia. All day long her thoughts had been wandering around many different ideas and the thought of Foster actually being Toby's son rather than his servant had entered her mind. "You brought Foster here to protect Ben."

"Yes."

"Why confess these dangerous truths to me?" Patricia asked. "Such truths, when discovered, only prove to become dangerous."

"Because," Toby answered in a careful voice, "if I die... you know the truth. Someone needs to know the truth. Someone needs to know that I'm not a monster." Toby looked up at Patricia. "When Lara was killed you immediately assumed that I was the killer."

"Yes, I did," Patricia confessed.

"I'm not a monster, Ms. McKay. My life was destroyed before I could begin living. Why? Because a carjacker pulled a gun on me, and after running him down, I fled the scene of the crime. If I had only stayed and waited for the police....

But fear is a cruel enemy," Toby finished in a tormented voice. "I was forced to become a monster—but I never wanted to become what I was forced to be."

Patricia wanted to feel pity for Toby but couldn't. A man walked his own path with the option of choice. Toby, she knew, could have changed the dark course he was pushed on at any time of his choosing. "Mr. Ells—"

"I can't tell Ben that I'm his brother. Not yet," Toby informed Patricia, allowing his tone to become rough and dangerous again. "I have been watching him. I'm not certain he would accept me as his brother. I need more time. If, in the end, I decide that Ben will reject me, I will take Foster and leave."

"I can accept that," Patricia said. "The question I was going to ask was this: Who is Karan? Is she part of your group?"

Toby shook his head no. "Karan showed up on her own. I'm not sure what her deal is."

Patricia didn't want to believe Toby's response, but her gut insisted the man was speaking the truth. "I—"

"Who is the killer, Ms. McKay?" Toby asked without allowing Patricia to complete her sentence. "Tell me and I will kill him or her. I will end this for all of us. It will be my present to Ben."

"Mr. Ells—"

"Is the killer Susie?" Toby asked as his eyes became dark and narrowed. "It's Susie, isn't it? I should have never allowed Foster to bring her onto our team. I assumed the girl was innocent—"

"The killer isn't Susie," Patricia assured Toby. "There was a time, earlier in the day, when my mind wondered if she was the killer, but she isn't."

"Then the killer is Karan. That's the only person who is left," Toby insisted.

"There's Foster."

"No!" Toby snapped to his feet and pointed a hard finger at Patricia. "My son isn't a killer."

"Calm down, Mr. Ells," Patricia ordered in a brave voice. "I know Foster isn't the killer."

"Then who?" Toby demanded. "Tell me."

"Not yet," Patricia replied and then simply pointed to the window. "In time, Mr. Ells, the killer will come out of the storm again—and then you'll know the truth. In the meantime, all we can do is watch…and wait."

chapter six

It was time to find out what Karan's story was. Patricia slipped into the creepy kitchen and spotted the woman standing next to an old kitchen sink peeling potatoes with a…knife. *Better not make her mad,* Patricia warned herself. Even though Trent was standing close to the back door and Ben was preparing what appeared to be a meatloaf on a separate kitchen counter, Patricia had no desire to see if Karan could stab her to death before anyone could stop her.

"Smells good," she said, smiling at Ben.

Ben kept his eyes on the ground hamburger meat that was sitting in an old green bowl. He picked up a bottle of garlic and added a few sprinkles. "We're having potato meatloaf," he explained in a tired voice. "Once Karan gets the potatoes peeled, I'll shred the potatoes and add them to the ground beef."

Trent felt his mouth begin to water. The guests lodging at the Dead and Breakfast weren't the only ones that were hungry. Donuts and sandwiches just weren't very filling. "Where is Mr. Ells?" he asked Patricia.

"Here," came Toby's gruff voice as he appeared in the kitchen doorway. Toby immediately spotted Foster and Susie sitting at the kitchen table together. Foster had his nose shoved into a cell phone. Susie was reading a book. "We're all accounted for," he told Trent, rotating his eyes over to Ben. Ben paid him no mind.

Patricia leaned against the kitchen counter that was now Karan's work station and waited for Toby to sit down. *How can I get this woman alone? I need to question her.* Patricia looked at Trent. The young cop was busy watching Ben work on the meatloaf. *That kid isn't going to let anyone leave this kitchen...I need to think.* "Karan?"

Karan shot a sour eye at Patricia. "What?" she asked in a voice dripping with ice.

"There is something I would like to discuss with you," Patricia said in a low voice. When Karan narrowed her eyes, Patricia drew in a deep breath and pretended to sound nervous. "You see, last night I had a...dream."

"A dream?" Karan asked without implying any element of interest.

"A dream." Patricia nodded, realizing she was catching everyone's attention. Foster looked up from his cell phone. Susie stopped reading her book. Ben stopped working on the meatloaf. Toby looked at her. Trent tossed a curious eye in her direction. *Perfect.* "I dreamed of a...murder. I...before I tell everyone my dream, I would like to see what you think first. Maybe we can talk in the hallway?"

"No one leaves this kitchen," Trent warned.

"The hallway that leads to the bathroom," Patricia clarified and pointed to the door that was hiding that short, shadowy hallway that led to the diseased bathroom she had reluctantly called Brian in. "I want to see what you think of the dream, Karan. I might...add the dream to the article I plan to write. Or who knows, maybe you can use it?" Patricia made a scared face. "I don't normally put much stock in dreams, but this one was so...spooky...and so real."

Karan lowered the knife she was holding. To Patricia's relief the woman nodded. "It's possible that you may have dreamed a real occurrence. After all, you are staying in the room Veronica Drakes was murdered in."

So, you do know a few facts, Patricia thought to herself. *You're not as innocent as you seem.* "Officer Trent, can we speak in the hallway? There is no exit."

"I…guess," Trent caved. "Make it quick. Gary will be here in about twenty minutes or so."

"You know us girls…chatter…chatter…chatter," Patricia said and then hurried to the closed door. "Karan?" Karan glanced around the kitchen and then followed after Patricia. Patricia opened the door and stepped into the dim, cold hallway. *This place is enough to make Herman Munster want to take a vacation.*

Karan stepped into the hallway behind Patricia and closed the door. "Let's talk in the bathroom," Karan ordered.

Patricia hesitated and then agreed. She doubted Karan would try to kill her. Besides, Patricia was pretty certain she knew who the real killer was. The only problem was…she didn't know if anyone here was connected to the killer. "Sure."

Karan followed Patricia into the dark, rotted bathroom and closed the door. "Okay, Ms. McKay, you brought me to talk. So. let's talk."

Patricia eased close to the bathroom sink. "I did have a dream, Karan," she confirmed. "I dreamed of Veronica Drakes. That's the truth. The dream was very scary and very vivid. But…yes, before I tell you about the dream, I would like to talk."

"You want to know if I killed Lara Braceton?" Karan asked Patricia in a flat tone. She folded her arms and leaned against the closed bathroom door. "Your little act this morning didn't fool anyone. I know you're an undercover cop."

"An undercover…cop?" Patricia asked in a shocked voice and then broke out laughing. "Karan, I'm not a cop. I'm dating a cop…but me…a cop?" Patricia imagined herself pulling over an old granny and writing out a parking ticket. "Too funny."

"Don't try and deceive me," Karan snapped. "Your claim to be a travel writer is weak—"

"I am a travel writer," Patricia insisted.

"I saw you arrive with Officer Horne last night. I saw you from my room window."

"That's because I was lost," Patricia explained. *Boy, was I way off with this one. She thinks I'm an undercover cop. The question is...why?* "Karan, why are you really here? Why did you travel to Ohio?"

"I've already told you I am a paranormal researcher—"

"That's what you claim," Patricia interrupted. "Are you really a paranormal investigator?"

Kara's eyes became dark and filled with cruel anger. "Yes."

"I can find out the truth. As a matter of fact, the cop I'm dating is hard at work as we speak digging into everyone's past," Patricia warned the other woman. "I have to make a call to Georgia in the next hour or so. I'm sure by then he'll have some very...interesting...information waiting for me to dice up."

"So, you're really not a cop—"

"I'm not a cop!" Patricia snapped. "Lady, my name is Patricia McKay. I'm a travel writer. For crying out, get online and look up the travel magazine I write for. My photo and name are under each article I write."

"My laptop...unfortunately...is missing. I haven't reported the theft...not yet" Karan confessed. "I assumed Foster took it."

"Why Foster?" Patricia asked.

"Foster has been snooping around ever since the murder last night," Karan explained. "He came to my room after Susie went to your room. He wanted to know if I had talked to Ben. I demanded he leave my room. A while later I decided to walk down to the kitchen and have a cup of hot tea before bed. When I returned to my room my laptop was missing." Karan's face loosened a little. A little hint of confusion and despair appeared. "Foster is young and handsome. I… assumed he was interested in me…personally. When I realized the truth, I kicked him out of my room."

Patricia glanced down at her hands. *So, Karan suffers from age-fright. Inside of her heart the woman still wants to believe she's young and beautiful. Not that she's a dog; she's a pretty woman, but it's clear age is taking its toll on her.* "Karan, why would Foster steal your laptop? Did you have any information stored on it that might have been…sensitive?"

Karan released an uneasy breath into the bathroom. "You're a cop—"

"I'm not a cop. I'm a travel writer—"

"Who has the mind of Nancy Drew. Yeah, and I was born yesterday, Ms. McKay," Karan snapped.

"You didn't seem to believe I was a cop earlier this morning. As a matter of fact—"

"Why would I let on that I know the truth?" Karan attacked Patricia. "If the killer realizes I know the truth I'm a dead woman. Can you understand that?"

"You know who the killer is?"

"Toby Ells!"

Patricia stared at Karan with clear, stern eyes. "Why do you believe Toby Ells is the killer?" she dared to ask.

"Toby Ells works for the mafia. He's here to locate a priceless chest of stolen jewels that's worth more money than your feeble imagination can understand," Karan said, feeling her voice become shaky.

Patricia steadied her mind. "You're aware of the history of this manor?"

"I know the facts, yes."

"Because you work for the private investigation company

Toby hired to locate his mother," Patricia pointed out and then waited patiently for Karan to respond.

Karan looked as if Patricia had slapped her across the face. "How did you...I mean, I..."

"And if you believe I'm an undercover cop, that means you're worried that the company you work for has sent someone to track you down. Why? Did you violate company policy, Karan...by, say, stealing sensitive information?" *Maybe the game of Clue isn't so bad after all. This case seems to be pulling together...so far. But there's no telling what sharp edges I might run into later on.*

Karan stared at Patricia with shocked eyes that quickly turned dark and vicious. "Mr. Hayster stabbed me in the back. I did all the work. All the research. I located Ben Grands. Me.... I searched out the truth. Months and months of tedious searching...countless hours...me. Not Mr. Hayster." Karan gritted her teeth. "Mr. Hayster found my work, and he betrayed me."

"How?" Patricia asked, pretending she knew who the mysterious Mr. Hayster was.

"He contacted Toby Ells and told him all about the missing treasure," Karan snapped. "Only the treasure he told Toby about was his brother, Ben Grands. He left out the part about the jewels. After all, Toby only wanted to find his brother...or did he?" Karan shook her head. "Toby is a very dangerous man. I believe he killed Lara Braceton because she knew the truth. Maybe Ben knows the truth too. Maybe Ben is next in line to die."

"Toby works for the mafia."

Karan's eyes grew large. "You...know?"

"I'm not a cop, Karan, but I do have my ways," Patricia explained without confessing that Toby himself had confessed his secrets to her. Sometimes a gal was blessed enough to find a few golden nuggets lying on the floor without having to dig for them. Life, after all, was never as neat and scripted as a murder game. No. Life was messy, disorganized, and full of unexpected twists and turns.

Karan pressed her back against the bathroom door. "Yes, Toby Ells does work for the mafia," she admitted. "The man is a vicious killer. He uses his position at the college he teaches at to smuggle in drugs and weapons."

"And I'm certain Foster assists him."

"Yes." Karan nodded.

Patricia felt a bad feeling creep into her heart. "Karan, you came here to steal the jewels, didn't you? You followed Toby Ells."

A look of absolute defeat struck Karan's face. "Ms. McKay, I was once a cop…a very good cop. But unfortunately, I began taking bribes. I suffered from an addiction—gambling, to be precise. My debts kept growing. I needed money." Karan lowered her eyes. "An undercover cop found me out. I was fired and put in prison for three years. When I left prison, no one would dare hire me…except for Mr. Hayster."

"Which tells me that Mr. Hayster isn't exactly an honest man."

"He's a killer," Karan said. "He uses his company to kill, threaten, and intimidate powerful people. I was hired to investigate the lives of corrupt politicians in order to create a systematic operation of blackmail." Karan's face began to drip with disgust. "Mr. Hayster suffered from a gambling addiction just like me, and he had very high debts."

"That's why he wanted the jewels?"

"Yes," Karan said. "Mr. Hayster may be a powerful man, but there are people who are far more powerful than he is."

"I'm sure there are."

Karan studied Patricia's face. "Because Toby Ells is a dangerous man, he was forced to seek help from Mr. Hayster instead of hiring an honest investigation firm."

Patricia slowly folded her arms. "I can understand that," she assured Karan and then took a second to gather her thoughts into an organized file. "So, you really believe Toby is the killer?"

"Who else could it be?" Karan insisted and then added, "I knew your little act this morning was fake." Karan glared at Patricia with careful eyes. "Mr. Hayster sent you to bring me back...after you kill Toby Ells."

"You're way off base, sister," Patricia assured Karan. "I don't know who this Mr. Hayster guy is, but I will. I'm not an undercover cop. And Toby Ells isn't the killer. You're striking out big time. But that doesn't mean that Mr. Hayster hasn't been able to reach his tentacles through this storm." Patricia leaned back against the bathroom sink and rubbed her chin. "This is a real mystery," she confessed, "but I think I might have a solid path to follow...maybe? I need to call my boyfriend."

Karan watched Patricia rubbing her chin. "Okay, smart girl, if you're not a cop...if you're a travel writer as you claim...then tell me why you just so happened to show up when everyone did. I don't believe in coincidences."

"Neither do I...sadly," Patricia sighed. "Neither do I." Patricia walked her eyes to the bathroom door. "I think we're going to be in for a lot of heartbreak, Karan."

"Heartbreak?"

"Listen to me," Patricia ordered. She stopped rubbing her chin, approached Karan, and gently took the woman's left hand. Karan tried to pull away but gave in. "I know you're not the killer. I know Toby Ells isn't the killer. I thought he was, but he isn't. For a while I even considered Susie—"

"Foster—"

"No," Patricia assured Karan, staring into the woman's hard eyes that were, to her relief, beginning to melt. "Karan, there is a killer loose...two, as a matter of fact—"

"Two?" Karan gasped.

Patricia nodded. "Two," she confirmed and let go of

Karan's hand. "I can't tell you who the two killers are...not yet—"

"Why not?"

"Because you might unintentionally give away the truth to everyone and we'll all be in danger," Patricia explained. "Right now, I need you to go back out into that kitchen and pretend you hate my guts. Complain about the dream I told you about. Make it seem like you're really annoyed with me. I'll play dumb."

"Why?" Karan insisted. "Ms. McKay—"

"Karan, my name is Patricia," Patricia said and offered a warm smile. "Let's not be enemies any longer, okay?" Patricia reached out and patted Karan's arm. "I promise to help you, but you have to be willing to quit fighting against the entire world."

"My life is in shambles. I need those jewels—"

"No, you need a friend," Patricia insisted and then opened the bathroom door. "Friends are worth more than money. Now, let me help you." Karan stared into a pair of eyes that held warmth and truth—a warmth and truth that she had not witnessed for a very long time. Without understanding how or why, Karan simply nodded yes and left the bathroom.

Gary Horne shook snow off his coat and then pulled a snow-soaked muffler hat off his head. "Boy, Trent, you're going to have a tough time getting home," he announced. "This is the worst storm I've ever seen. I'm sorry I'm so late. Getting here was a real chore."

Trent quickly tossed on a muffler and a pair of thick gloves. "Who cares?" he told Gary moving toward the front door. "All I want is a hot meal, a hot shower, and my bed."

Gary nodded. "I can understand that," he said and then

pointed toward the front room. "What's the news on our locked-up chickens?"

"Nothing," Trent replied, offering a simple summary. "It's been quiet all day. Everyone is in the front room. Dinner has just ended. Mr. Grands cooked a meatloaf, but I didn't get very much of it."

A grin swept across Gary's face. "We cops are underappreciated. But that's going to change."

"Yeah, when cows fly over the moon," Trent huffed as he yanked open the front door. "See you tomorrow morning."

"Yeah…be careful going home," Gary called out. He watched Trent vanish into the storm and then fought to close the front door.

Patricia spotted Gary closing the front door and then walked back into the front room. "Well, Officer Horne is here," she announced.

"Oh joy," Karan snapped, sitting in a reading chair holding a book. As far as everyone was concerned—even Ben —Karan still despised the ground Patricia walked on.

Before Patricia could respond, Gary appeared. "How is everyone tonight?" he asked in a tone that didn't seem very friendly. "Trent told me today went by without any problems. Let's see to it that tonight matches today's attitude."

Patricia walked over to the old cobblestone fireplace and began warming her hands. She hated how the front room felt like a funeral parlor. The screaming, tormented, icy winds outside didn't add any color to the situation, but what could she do? "We're all very tired, Officer Horne. It's been a long day. I for one would like to retire to my room and rest."

"I second that," Foster piped up. "We're not prisoners, you know."

"My lawyer will not be pleased to know that we're being held against our will," Toby added in a stern tone.

"The guests do need to rest," Ben supported Toby.

"I insist we be allowed to go to our rooms," Karan plowed in.

"I agree," Susie finished.

"Whoa...whoa...," Gary hollered. "Everyone take a deep breath and calm down. I realize the hour is late. I was just going to suggest everyone go up to their rooms."

"Good," Karan snapped. She tossed a quick eye at Patricia and then stood up. "I will be in my room."

"As we all will," Toby added.

"And I'll be sitting in the chair at the end of the hallway, so no funny stuff," Gary ordered. "Chief Winchester will be here in the morning—well, more around noon. When the storm lets up, he'll probably let everyone leave. Storm is supposed to start weakening tomorrow afternoon sometime. Plows will come out then."

"I won't be leaving anytime soon," Toby announced.

Ben sighed. "I'm afraid I will insist that all guests check out and leave," he told Toby. "The Dead and Breakfast is going to be closed...for good."

"Suits me," Susie stated in an ugly tone. "I'll be in my room. The quicker I get back to California the better." Susie charged toward the staircase with her book. "By the way, Mr. Graves, it would be nice if you brought a nice hot tea up to my room. I am still a guest, you know."

Ben nodded. "Sure. I'll bring everyone a hot drink before I turn in."

"No, you won't—"

"Yes, I will," Ben snapped at Gary. "It's been a very cold and trying day, Officer Horne. My guests deserve to be treated nicely."

"One of you could be a killer," Gary snapped back.

"No one here is a killer," Ben assured him.

"And how do you know that? Are you an expert, Mr. Graves? Huh? Are you?" Gary stepped toward Ben in a threatening manner and pointed a hard finger at him. "Need I remind you that your niece was stabbed to death in this very room?"

"I'm very aware of where and how my niece died, Officer Horne," Ben growled, showing a sudden renewed strength that shocked and pleased Patricia. "I'm also aware that all the guests came downstairs when ordered…not from outside. Foster was with Patricia upstairs when the murder took place and the rest of the guests were in their rooms—"

"So they say—"

"So I know," Ben snapped. "No guest showed any signs of being outside. But even if one of them had managed to slip outside, I would have known."

"How?" Gary demanded.

"I…." Ben tossed Patricia a sorrowful eye. "I'm sorry, but I lied to you, Ms. McKay, when you asked me if there are any hidden doors or hallways in this cursed manor," he explained. "There are a few hidden hallways. You see," Ben said, walking over to a red chair and sitting down, "when I arrived, I explored every inch of this manor. I wasn't exactly walking blind, either."

"Walking blind? What does that mean?" Gary asked, becoming very upset with Ben. "Are you hiding something?"

"My mother left me this manor and she knew every inch of this place by heart," Ben explained, returning to a calm tone. "Before my mother died, she told where every hidden hallway was located. I know about places that even my wife isn't aware of…places I figured she was better off not knowing about."

Patricia looked at Gary. The man's face twisted into a tight knot. *Wow, this guy is turning redder than a firecracker.* "No harm, no foul, Mr. Graves," she said. "After all, this is your property."

"There is harm!" Gary yelled. "You withheld information from the police. I have every right to arrest you."

"So, arrest me," Ben told Gary, remaining calm. "My

lawyer will have me free within hours." Ben looked up at Gary. "I'll also have a lawsuit against the city of Whispering Hills for false arrest."

"You withheld information—"

"No officer of the law asked me about any hidden hallways," Ben informed Gary as if he were a stupid child. "How is revealing the truth now construed as withholding information from the police when the police never directly approached me with a clear and concise question concerning hidden hallways?"

Gary began to speak but then backed down. His eyes dripped with rage. "You just make sure you tell the truth from now on, Mr. Graves," he warned.

Ben sighed. "To return back to our original conversation," he told Gary. "I happen to know none of the guests killed my niece because behind each room upstairs is a hidden hallway—along with other hidden hallways I will not mention."

"How does that prove—"

"Listen," Ben scolded Gary. He leaned back in his chair and closed his eyes. "My niece was killed in this room—"

"I know that," Gary hissed.

"And my niece was rooming with Susie."

All eyes turned to Susie. "I didn't kill Lara," Susie cried out.

"But someone did," Ben stated. He slowly opened his eyes. "Ms. McKay said that Lara left her room and soon after she was found dead."

"Yeah, we know that," Gary insisted, showing a poison impatience that only youth and arrogance could possess.

"About…twenty minutes passed, Ms. McKay, between the time Lara left your room and you heard her cry out?" Ben asked.

"Twenty to thirty." Patricia nodded.

"I was outside moving Ms. McKay's vehicle, but I…well, I

got the back tires stuck by accident. I had a view of the front of manor…especially the front door, the entire time."

"What does this have to do with anything? Lara Braceton was killed inside, not outside," Gary demanded. "Unless… you're the killer. Maybe you are?"

"No, I didn't kill my niece," Ben replied without losing his temper. "If you would let me finish, I can prove all of my guests, along with myself, are innocent." Ben fought back a yawn. "I've had all day to get my thoughts together and draw my own conclusions." Ben pointed at Toby. "At first, I believed Mr. Ells killed Lara, and then I began wondering if Karan or Susie matched up. But then I realized a very important fact."

"What?" Gary asked in a voice that seemed venomous rather than professional.

"The hallways," Ben explained and pointed to the fireplace. "Lara's body…the way she was lying face down on the floor. Her back was to the fireplace, and there happens to be a hidden doorway next to the fireplace that leads into a hallway that goes upstairs."

All eyes locked onto the wall next to the fireplace. "I don't see a door. All I see is an old wall," Susie complained. "Mr. Graves, this is no time for a joke—"

"Hence the word *hidden*," Ben cut Susie off. He stood up, walked across the room, and placed both of his hands on the old wall. Without saying a word, he pressed his hands forward. To Patricia's amazement the wall began to push back…but not the entire wall, just a portion of the wall that resembled a door. Cold, icy air began flooding from the hidden doorway along with a strange, dusty smell.

"The room was cold, of course, when I arrived because the killer escaped through the front door, so I didn't think anything of the cold at the time. But, as you can all see, the door opened without the slightest sound…and now there is a smell…a very old smell."

Patricia sniffed the air. The odor coming from the hidden doorway smelled like…the faint scent of kerosene. "I smell it."

"Smells like…kerosene," Karan spoke up, sniffing the air. "Faint, but distinguishable."

"I agree." Toby nodded.

Ben turned to face everyone. "There were signs of a struggle," he continued. "Right, Ms. McKay?"

Patricia stepped close to Ben. "Yes, Lara's body did show signs that she fought with the killer before being killed." *Which doesn't make any sense if the killer sneaked up behind her… which means my theory is right: there are two killers.* "It was very clear to me that Lara did fight with a killer."

"And none of my guests show any signs of harm," Ben told Gary and then closed the hidden door. The door closed without a sound, which was surprising. In a house this old it should have creaked and moaned louder than the howling winds outside. "Whoever killed my niece stepped out from this hidden door and stabbed her. Stabbed her while she was fighting with someone."

"That doesn't prove that all of the guests are innocent," Gary claimed, showing a clear and present determination to prove that one of the guests staying at Ben's manor was filled with guilt. "Anyone could have found that old door—"

"Ms. McKay, try to open the door," Ben asked.

"Sure." Patricia stepped up to the wall and placed her hands where Ben instructed her to. "Press?" Ben nodded. Patricia, assuming she could open the hidden door without any objection, suddenly found herself struggling to push the door open. "It's…stuck. I can't open it."

"That's because you have to know how," Ben explained. "Please move away, Ms. McKay." Patricia stepped to the side. Ben looked at everyone and then placed his hands back on the wall. "There is a latch that you must disengage—a hidden latch that is very difficult to locate with your fingers." Ben located the latch and opened the door again. "The person who killed my niece knew how to find the latch. I don't think a single guest knew about this door, let alone knew about the latch."

Gary glared at Ben with hard eyes. "That doesn't prove a thing, Mr. Graves. A police officer officer always assumes the worst before accepting the best. In my eyes everyone is guilty."

Ben's hidden revelation caused Patricia's mind to start stirring a few more ingredients into the deadly mystery. *Lara was struggling with one of the killers... and the second killer stepped out from the hidden door and murdered her...and the person Lara was fighting with escaped through the front door...while the killer went back into the walls.* "Ben, when did you get my SUV unstuck?"

"Oh, I'd say about twenty minutes after I left you and Lara," Ben said. "It took me a minute because I backed into a snowdrift."

"And you saw no one?" Patricia asked.

"Not from the outside," Ben explained.

"And there was only one set of snow tracks leading to the front door," Patricia mused. She turned and faced the hidden door. "Ben—"

"This hallway branches off into the kitchen," Ben told Patricia, assuming that's the question the smart young woman was going to ask.

"Okay," Patricia nodded, "thanks, Ben. That answers my question."

"What question?" Gary demanded. "Withholding information from the police is a crime."

Patricia locked her eyes on Gary. "It's possible, Officer Horne—"

"That there are two killers!" Susie exclaimed. "It doesn't take a genius to figure out what Patricia is thinking!" Susie turned to Foster. "I don't want to go up to my room now. Please stay with me."

Foster tossed a sour eye at Susie. "You're kidding, right?"

Susie felt her heart shatter. "I was hoping…that you were a nice guy."

"You can stay with me," Karan told Susie in a gentle voice that shocked everyone. "I know you're scared. So am I."

Toby threw a displeased eye at Foster but didn't say a word. Instead, he looked at Patricia and then focused on Ben. "I'll be upstairs, Mr. Graves. You can bring me a tea later… and maybe then we can talk."

Patricia watched Toby walk away. Foster quickly followed. "Everyone, upstairs," Gary ordered. "No drinks…just get upstairs."

"My room is downstairs, Officer Horne," Ben clarified as he closed the hidden door. "And as far as the drinks go, I will serve all of my guests a late-night coffee or tea with or without your permission. We are not prisoners. If you treat us as such my lawyer will have your badge." Ben turned to Patricia. "Come on, Ms. McKay, I will walk you up to your room."

Patricia looked at Gary with a careful eye and then allowed Ben to walk her upstairs. "Any more secrets?" she whispered

"Some," Ben confessed under his breath but didn't speak again until he was safely locked in a spooky room holding very dangerous secrets.

<h1 align="right">chapter seven</h1>

"You're a very sneaky person, Ben," Patricia said as she paced around the spooky room Ben had assigned her. "I wonder what else you're keeping from me." Patricia paused and studied Een's tired face. "While I've been playing Nancy Drew all day, you've been holding out on me."

"Well, your little act this morning didn't exactly fool anyone," Ben pointed out. "I played along, but I could tell Toby and Karan were wise to it. I figured I needed to start doing some of my own thinking."

"Okay, so trying to make everyone believe I was dumb wasn't so smart. I was hoping to...oh, forget it. What's important is that my little act did pay off. Both Toby and Karan opened up to me and spilled out a whole lot of truth." Patricia stepped close to the large bed standing in the middle of the room, studied the bed curtain wrapped around the bed, and then turned to face Ben. "Sit down while I reveal what was told to me today and—" Before Patricia could finish her sentence her cell phone rang. "That might be Brian...one second."

"I'm not going anywhere." Ben sat down on the green

couch and rested his legs while Patricia fished her phone out of her purse.

"Hey, Brian…I know I should have called, but I figured you would call me when you had something," Patricia said in a quick tone.

"I don't have very much gold to give you," Brian told her in a tired voice. "I've had the mayor kicking at me all day, but I did manage to do some digging in between being hollered at and wondering if I was going to get canned, but the chief really stood by and—"

"Seems like the mayor was just wanting to yell a little more."

"Basically," Brian agreed and then picked up a brown file off his desk. "Okay, Patricia, ready your ears because I'm exhausted and you're my last chore…uh, call for the day."

Patricia could clearly hear that Brian was exhausted and didn't take offense to his statement. "You don't seem very worried anymore."

"Well, I'm not as worried," Brian explained. "The names you gave me don't connect to a killer—at least not in my professional opinion. The only bad dude on the list is Toby Ells. That guy is real bad news, but he's not a killer. He's killed a few men but each time a jury found that he killed in self-defense."

"I had a talk with Mr. Ells, today, Brian. I cleared him from my list."

Brian opened the folder and pulled out a piece of paper. "Smart girl," he said, "because I have a suspect in mind. But first let me clear the guest list you gave me." Patricia waited while Brian cleared his throat. "Karan…ex-cop, went to prison for taking bribes…ended up working for a shady investigation company run by a crook."

"Yep, Karan confessed her past to me."

Brian sighed. "Okay…Susie…college girl…no criminal

record…spent a little time in a rehab center for drug use… nothing major."

"Susie is clear," Patricia agreed.

Brian shook his head and continued. "Foster…Foster is—"

"Toby Ells's son."

Brian tossed down the paper he was holding. "Why did you ask me to investigate these people when you have all the answers?"

Patricia giggled a little. "I guess I got ahead of you a little, honey…sorry."

Brian melted into Patricia's sweet giggle. "You're forgiven," he promised and then put on a serious voice. "Did you investigate Ben Graves's wife?"

Patricia stopped giggling and looked at Ben. Ben was staring at her with curious eyes. "Not yet…but my gut is telling me the woman is involved."

"Patricia, Melinda Graves isn't in Michigan. Her credit card trail shows that she's there in Whispering Hills."

Patricia sighed. "I was afraid of that."

Brian picked up his coffee. "Melinda Graves rented a room at the Whispering Hills Hotel. And get this—" Brian took a sip of coffee. "—the only other guest registered at the hotel is a man named. Edmund Hayster. Edmund Hayster—"

"Is the man who owns the shady investigation company Karan worked for…the same company Toby hired to locate his mother," Patricia whispered.

"Seems like you have this case all figured out," Brian told Patricia and then added in a careful voice, "I still have to do some more digging, but for now it seems that all the guests are in the clear. But Patricia, Ben Graves might not be in the clear—"

"Ben is…but the other mentioned person is not," Patricia told Brian, feeling her heart break for Ben. Ben was such a sweet man…strange…a little creepy…but very sweet. "Is that all you have for me?"

"Until tomorrow."

"Okay," Patricia said, "but don't expect to go home just yet. I need one favor before you call it a night."

"Patricia, it's been a twelve-hour workday and—"

"One person," Patricia begged.

Brian let out a tired breath. "Anything for you," he told her in a caring voice. "Let me have the name."

"Gary Horne. He's a local cop."

"Gary Horne...got it. Give me an hour," Brian told Patricia and then added: "When you get home remind me to chain you to your barn."

"Remind me to punch Edna in the nose," Patricia told him and then ended the call. She put her cell phone away and walked over to Ben and sat down on the couch next to him. "Ben?"

"What did your cop friend have to say?"

"That everyone is in the clear as far as he can tell...except for one very specific person," Patricia explained in a low voice.

"Gary Horne."

"Gary Horne is a suspect, yes—"

"The killer?"

"No," Patricia answered, feeling a heavy sadness enter her voice. "Ben, you showed everyone the hidden door downstairs to help prove their innocence, but I believe you wanted me to see the hidden door more than anyone else...right?"

Ben stiffened and sat very quiet for a few minutes. "I didn't want to believe it was possible...not Melinda," he finally spoke in a tormented voice. "All day I kept replaying the murder in my mind. All day I kept trying to pin the murder on one of the guests, but no amount of wishful thinking could overpower the plain and simple, logical truth. Each guest, except for Foster, was upstairs—and Foster was with you. No guest could have slipped downstairs and then back upstairs without being seen unless they used the hidden hallway…but how? Which guest knew about it—and how to disengage the latch?"

"No one," Patricia confirmed. She reached out and patted Ben's arm. "Ben, how is your marriage? Please…I have to ask, so don't hate me."

Ben turned his now tearful eyes and looked into Patricia's sweet, caring face. "Melinda didn't go to see her sick sister. She…left me, Ms. McKay. I…Melinda has left me before but has always come home. I was hoping that would be the case this time around." Ben shook his head. "She seemed so attracted to this cursed manor. She began creating ways to turn it into a gold mine…she was so excited. But then…I don't know what happened."

"Take your time, Ben."

Ben looked down at his hands. "It was Melinda's idea that you come here and write about this manor. I wasn't very happy. All I wanted to do was find—"

"All the jewels?" Patricia asked.

Ben's eyes grew wide. "You know?"

"Karan told me."

"Karan knows?" Ben asked in a shaky voice.

Patricia nodded. "Yes…and I'm certain other people besides Karan know…maybe even Lara knew…and that's why she was killed."

A painful moan left Ben's throat. "Veronica Drakes's husband was a monster," he whispered to Patricia. "I admit that Henry Graves was no prince, but he wasn't a monster. Theodore Drakes. He killed his wife in order to destroy Henry."

"But there's more to the story, right?" Patricia asked, daring to glance at the corner Veronica Drakes's body had been found in.

Ben slowly nodded. "What I'm about to say is based off speculation…at least, up until a few months ago."

"Start from the beginning."

Ben sat back and rubbed his thin face. "During the Civil War both the Union and Confederate armies raided many homes and stole a great amount from countless families." Ben glanced at Patricia. "Maybe General Lee did sabotage the entire Confederate Army at Gettysburg...maybe he didn't. It seems strange that a man of his skill would force his army to walk into enemy fire. And rumors were some of his most valued officers did not have their men in position before the attack began. But that's a piece of foggy mystery that will remain hidden in the graves of the past."

"I suppose so," Patricia agreed in a sad voice.

"Anyway," Ben continued, "the Union Army, after the war, located a rare shipment of jewels that had been stolen from somewhere in Europe—we're talking about millions upon millions of dollars' worth of jewels that countless treasure hunters have searched for throughout the decades. An unnamed general in the Union Army took the jewels north and entrusted them to Theodore Drakes."

"An unnamed general?"

"That's the way history is sometimes. Sometimes there are missing pieces," Ben explained.

"Yes, it does seem to be that. Please continue."

Ben rubbed his weary eyes. "The jewels were entrusted to Theodore Drakes because Theodore Drakes was planning to create his own private army...kind of like a shadow government that is poisoning our land today. Many high-ranking officials were part of the scheme."

"But?" Patricia asked.

"Henry Graves entered the scene and exposed Theodore Drakes with the help of Veronica Drakes." Ben folded his arms and stared across the spooky room. "Henry Graves basically dug his own grave...and so did Veronica Drakes. They pushed a wild lion into a corner."

"I suppose they did," Patricia agreed.

Ben nodded toward the far corner. "Theodore Drakes strangled his wife to death with a piece of rope. Henry Graves found her body. Rumor is he killed himself after jumping out of that boarded up window, but that's not the way the story really goes."

"Henry Graves escaped the fall," Patricia stated, remembering her dream.

"Yes," Ben said, nodding. "He escaped with his life and the jewels. However, in time, Theodore Drakes captured Henry and...tortured the man to death after Henry refused to confess where he hid the jewels." Ben sighed. "Veronica Drakes is my relative...but Henry cursed her. If only Henry would have stayed away...stayed away from those jewels..." Ben lifted his eyes and looked at Patricia. "I do want to have the last laugh...on everyone, Ms. McKay. My entire life has been cursed...and I blame it on Henry Graves."

"Why?"

"Because Henry was the reason Veronica Drakes was killed," Ben answered in an angry voice. "According to the history report I managed to compile—from old eyewitness accounts, from statements Theodore Drakes made himself before being hung for treason—Veronica was planning on divorcing her husband and marrying Henry. But, as I mentioned, Henry was no prince. The man may not have been a killer, but he surely wasn't a prince. If only...." Ben sighed. "Yes, if only...."

Patricia struggled to understand Ben's reasoning but failed. Each heart held its own mysterious chambers of pain and misery and it seemed that Ben was determined to pin all of his pain on Henry Graves rather than Theodore Drakes. Patricia clearly couldn't look into the past and see all the details, but she figured that Ben assumed that if Henry Graves wouldn't have entered the scene, Veronica Drakes would have lived and whatever curse Ben believed was following him would never have been allowed to leave its grave.

The heart is the greatest mystery of all and sometimes…the heart just doesn't make any sense to a pair of strange eyes, Patricia thought. *Who can understand the heart of a poet or the mind of a madman?* "Ben, did Henry hide the jewels in this manor?"

"Yes," Ben confessed. "Why do you think Griffin North turned this manor into a nursing home? He was searching for the jewels but needed a disguise. Having a bunch of elderly people around to make the world think he was a prince while searching for the jewels was a good scheme…but Griffin failed."

Patricia stood up and rubbed the back of her neck. "Ben, when did Melinda change?"

"Couple of days ago," Ben explained in a troubled voice. "I don't know what happened. We had…an argument. I always seemed to find a way to get on her nerves somehow. That specific day I had failed to work on an upstairs toilet. Anyway, Melinda left the manor to go into town and buy some groceries…or so she said, leaving me alone. When she returned…." Ben walked over to the bed and kicked at the floor. "She packed up her things and left. She claimed she was going to stay with her sister, but she's in town at the local hotel. I saw her truck."

Patricia felt Ben's heart break. She walked over to the man and touched his arm. "Ben, listen to me," she pleaded. "It is my belief that Edmund Hayster is the mastermind behind this nightmare."

"Edmund Hayster?"

"Edmund Hayster owns a private investigation company that…that…." Patricia bit down on her lower lip. *Forgive me, Mr. Ells, for spilling the beans, but Ben has to know.* "Toby Ells hired the investigation company Edmund Hayster owns to locate his mother…*your* mother, Ben."

"My…mother?" Ben asked as if Patricia had socked him in the gut.

"Ben…Toby Ells believes that you are his brother," Patricia confessed and then winced. "Forgive me, Mr. Ells. You can kill me later."

"My brother?" Ben asked and then began shaking his head no. "No, that's not possible. I don't have any siblings. My mother would have told me—"

"Would she?" Patricia asked. "Ben, Toby Ells works for the mafia…well, he did. He's a hard and dangerous man…well, he was. Maybe your mother didn't want you to know about him. Maybe your mother wanted you to burn down this cursed manor and end the nightmare." Patricia touched Ben's arm again "Ben, did your mother know about the jewels?"

"How could she have not known?" Ben asked in a painful voice. He sighed. "Veronica Drakes had a child, as I mentioned to you before. Theodore Drakes believed the child belonged to Henry Graves, but that wasn't the case. My bloodline comes from Veronica Drakes." Ben walked back to the couch and sat down. "Theodore Drakes was hung in his early eighties. I think he confessed the entire truth to the child he thought belonged to Henry Graves…but finally realized belonged to him. I don't understand how else the mystery about the jewels could have spread."

Patricia checked the time. The hour was getting late. *So much for sleep. I have to wake up my extra thinking cap and get to work.*

"That's my stance on this case, Brian," Patricia said into her cell phone.

"I can't argue," Brian stated, staring at a piece of paper containing some very dangerous information concerning

Gary Horne. "Gary Horne transferred to Whispering Hills last year."

"Around the time Karan began her investigation," Patricia whispered to herself.

"Gary Horne has a bad rap sheet," Brian continued. "I don't know how he's still a cop."

"Yeah…." Patricia thought of Chief Winchester. "You know, Brian, I had a bad feeling about Gary from the start, but I wasn't able to put my finger on why. Gary pulled me over right when I arrived in Whispering Hills. He claimed he saw me take the turnoff, but maybe he was waiting. And he asked for my name very quickly, but he didn't ask for my driver's license or any other form of identification. He then offered to let me follow his patrol car to this spooky old manor. I should have known something was fishy."

"Don't kick yourself. Patricia. You were thrown into a bad situation."

"Yeah…." Patricia closed her eyes and saw her warm—safe—farmhouse appear. "Brian, I think you better contact the Ohio State Police…or someone…and get them out here. My gut is telling me that Edmund Hayster has bought off the entire Whispering Hills police department."

"I'm on it…but Patricia, that snowstorm you're trapped in was forecast to weaken by tomorrow but a new storm front is moving in right behind it. Just saw the latest weather report," Brian explained. "Weather station is calling it a double whammy. Nothing in your area is moving." Brian gulped down some coffee. "I'll make a few calls, but without any proof…right now all that will happen is that a call will be made to Chief Winchester—"

"Who will deny everything."

"You got it, good-looking," Brian confirmed. "I can't call out the Staties unless I have solid proof. Besides, we don't know what type of connection Chief Winchester has with the state. He may have friends in high places. Who knows at this point?"

"What you're saying is that I need to catch a few rats in order to close down a corrupt town."

"Bingo," Brian said. He was worried sick about Patricia, but there was nothing that could be done on his end. Patricia was trapped in a vicious snowstorm and he couldn't get to her. "Patricia, I know that you're a brilliant, clever woman, but you're on your own…so think smart…keep your gun in your hands…and shoot first."

"I don't need bullets just yet. Right now, I need some cheese." Patricia glanced over at Ben, who was standing beside the bed lost in his own thoughts. "I'll call you every hour on the hour. If I fail to call you…call in the State Police."

"I'll be beside the phone," Brian promised.

Patricia sadly ended the call and walked over to Ben. "You better go talk to Toby, Ben. I'll stay here in the room and try to think of a plan."

"How can that man be my brother? No. It's impossible," Ben objected. "I'm certain my mother would have told me if—"

"Ben, there is only one way to find out."

Ben stared at Patricia and then let his head drop. "I guess you're right, Ms. McKay…Patricia," he whispered and then slowly raised his sorrowful eyes. "You live a very interesting life. It's too bad you have to become involved with mine."

Patricia took Ben's hands in her own. "Ben, God works in so many mysterious ways. Each path I walk helps me grow as a person, and in the end, I do grow. And I also make new, special friends. I was upset that Edna sent me here, but because of you, now I'm glad I came."

Ben felt a weak smile touch his eyes. "So am I," he assured Patricia and then looked around the room. "This is a cursed manor. As soon as I find the jewels, we will split the money and then burn this place down," he promised and then left the room, leaving Patricia all alone.

Patricia ran her hands through her hair and began pacing back and forth. "Think," she begged her mind. "You have all the facts, but how do we catch the killers? And who is the killer? Did Gary Horne kill Lara…or did Melinda Graves? Or maybe Edmund Hayster?" Patricia paced over to the boarded-up window and placed her hands on a cold, rotted board. "Lara fought with someone, but the killer sneaked up behind her. Someone knew about the hidden door and that someone wasn't Gary Horne. Gary Horne was shocked to see Ben show everyone the hidden door…so that leaves Melinda Graves."

As Patricia talked her thoughts through, Gary watched Ben knock on Toby Ells's door. Toby answered the knock a few seconds later and invited Ben into his room. As soon as Ben was out of sight and the hallway was silent, a shadow sneaked up behind Gary.

"Go kill the writer," a voice hissed in an urgent voice. "She knows the truth…and then kill Ben. They have to die."

Gary spun around and saw Melinda Graves standing behind him holding a gun that had a silencer attached to the barrel. The woman was wearing a cruel, vicious face devoid of life, love, and compassion. Gary saw a woman with dead eyes staring at him. But so what? Edmund Hayster was signing his paychecks, not Melinda.

"I take orders from Edmund, old lady." Gary glanced at the long gray robe Melinda was wearing—a robe that matched the ugly woman's long gray hair—and shook his head. "You look ridiculous."

"You almost let Lara escape. If I hadn't killed her, she would have gotten away," Melinda hissed, ignoring Gary's insult. "Edmund is not happy with you!" Melinda reached out and snatched up Gary's right coat sleeve. Ugly, deep claw marks appeared on the man's arm. "Look at that."

Gary snatched his arm away from Melinda and pushed down his coat sleeve. "Lara caused her own death. She refused to cooperate with me. She got what was coming to her."

"You nearly cost us everything," Melinda scolded Gary. "Go kill the writer and then kill Ben."

"I take orders from—"

"These are orders from Edmund," Melinda warned him. "You can call him yourself."

Gary looked into Melinda's cold eyes and saw that the woman was speaking the truth. "Well, it's a perfect night for murder," he told her. "I might just have myself a little fun and kill—"

"Patricia McKay and Ben Grands," Melinda ordered Gary. "No one else dies unless they get in the way. Chief Winchester is covering up Lara's death…and we can cover up two more deaths…but we can't cover up—"

"I get it," Gary growled under his breath. "I'll take out the smart-mouthed girl and the old man."

"I'll be behind the walls watching," Melinda told him. "Patricia McKay is in her room. Follow me."

Gary followed Melinda downstairs and slipped through the hidden door Ben had revealed to everyone. He then proceeded to follow the woman down a cold, stone tunnel that ended at a flight of stone steps. Melinda paused, checked her gun, and then, before Gary could act, she suddenly spun around and ended his life with a single bullet.

"One down…many to go," she grinned. "After I kill Ms. McKay and my husband, I will kill you, Edmund…and the treasure will be all mine."

Melinda checked the watch that was attached to her wrist. "It's getting late. I have to hurry." Melinda left Gary's body lying where it was and hurried up the stone steps and maneuvered down a dark hallway that ended behind Patricia's room. A single door that led into the closet housed in Patricia's room called Melinda's name. Melinda crept through the door on dangerous, silent legs and eased into the closet. *I'll shoot her and then go kill Ben,* she thought, preparing to burst out of the closet and shoot Patricia dead.

Patricia didn't hear or see Melinda enter the closet. She had her back to the closet and was feeling the rotted board covering the window. But suddenly something—something powerful— told her to run for her purse and grab the gun Brian had stashed inside it. A voice…an angel…Patricia didn't know. All she knew was that a powerful surge of urgency rushed into her heart. Without taking a mere second to try and understand what was happening, Patricia dashed to the bed, snatched up her purse, and managed to retrieve the hidden gun inside right when Melinda broke free from the closet. Patricia immediately dropped down behind the bed just as Melinda fired two bullets at her. Realizing that she had missed her target, Melinda ran for the bed, hoping to shoot down a trapped rabbit. What the evil woman didn't know was that the trapped rabbit had a gun.

"There's no sense in fighting the inevitable—" Melinda hissed, but then she crashed to a stop when Patricia rolled out from behind the bed and fired off three bullets. The bullets tore into Melinda's body—and ended the woman's miserable life.

Ben heard the gunshots. "Let's go!" he yelled at Toby, running out of Toby's room. "Ms. McKay!" Toby followed Ben to Patricia's room, pulled his brother back, and kicked open the door. Ben rushed inside and then stopped. Patricia was lying on the floor holding a gun…and his wife was lying close by…dead. "Melinda…no…."

Patricia watched Ben walk over to his dead wife, drop down onto his knees, and begin to cry. Toby put a hand on his brother's shoulder and bowed his head. "Are you okay, Ms. McKay?" he asked.

Patricia crawled to her legs. As she did a warm hand

touched her shoulder—a hand that, she knew, belonged to an angel. *An angel has been with me in this nightmare the entire time…watching me…protecting me*, Patricia realized as she struggled to calm her nerves. "I'm so sorry. I had no choice but to shoot her. She was shooting at me."

"I know," Toby told Patricia in a low voice. "It's always self-defense…leaving the innocent no choice but to become monsters."

Foster, Susie, and Karan came rushing into the room. When they saw Melinda lying on the floor each person stopped in their tracks and looked at Patricia. "It's Ben's wife, and she's dead," Patricia explained in a sorrowful voice. "Where is Officer Horne?"

"He's not out in the hallway," Foster told Patricia.

Patricia eyed the closet. "Melinda entered my room through that closet. Mr. Ells…will you please come with me? Everyone else please remain with Ben."

Toby removed his hand from Ben's shoulder and followed Patricia to the closet. Patricia eased her head into the dark space and spotted a hidden door that was standing open. She quickly checked her gun and then looked back at Toby. To her relief, rather than fear, she saw the man reach into his jacket and pull out a gun of his own. "Ready?" Toby nodded. "Here we go."

Ben raised his head and watched Patricia and Toby vanish into the closet. "Why?" he asked Melinda. "Why? The curse was mine, not yours, but you…you brought a curse upon yourself…." Ben wiped tears from his eyes and then asked Foster, Susie, and Karan to go find a sheet to cover his wife's body with.

Patricia didn't hear Ben ask for a funeral sheet. Instead, she crept into a cold, dark hallway made of stone. "Mr. Ells—"

Toby reached into his jacket pocket and retrieved a

penlight. "I'm right behind you," he said, turning on the penlight.

"Thanks," Patricia whispered, grateful to have a bit of light. She squeezed her gun and kept moving down the hallway until it ended at a set of stone steps. "Well...down we go," she whispered to Toby and carefully began descending each stone step. Toby followed without saying a word. He had an uneasy feeling that Patricia was going to find an unpleasant surprise at the bottom of the stairs. Patricia had the same uneasy feeling. It wasn't long before her uneasy feeling became reality. "Oh my...it's Officer Horne," she whispered, reaching the bottom of the stairs and spotting Gary's body lying on the floor.

Toby moved past Patricia, checked Gary's neck for a pulse, and then shook his head. "He's dead."

"I assumed," Patricia said in a miserable voice.

"You should be happy. The killers are all dead," Toby told Patricia in a voice that was still hard and cold. He stood up and turned to face Patricia. "What's the matter?"

"Mr. Ells, Edmund Hayster is part of this game," Patricia explained. "Maybe Melinda Graves is dead...I didn't want to help her...and maybe Gary Horne is dead, but we still have one more killer running loose."

"Edmund Hayster? I don't understand."

"Maybe I can help you to understand," a voice said.

Patricia spun around and spotted Karan standing on the stone stairs. "Yes, maybe you can, Karan."

Karan focused her eyes entirely on Toby and began revealing deep, hidden secrets. "That's the way of this story, Mr. Ells," she said when she finished. "You can believe me or—"

"I believe you," Toby assured Karan, feeling anger drip from his voice. "Edmund betrayed me. I'll kill him."

"We have to find the man first," Patricia told Toby. She

lowered her gun and looked around. "This place is creepy. Let's go out into the front room and talk there."

"Fine," Toby agreed.

"Okay." Karan nodded.

"All we have to do is open the door." Patricia walked over to the hidden door separating the stone hallway from the front room and began fiddling with it. To her relief the door opened up without any argument. "You don't have to pop the latch from this side," she explained and began pushing the door open. *How are we going to catch Edmund Hayster and prove Chief Winchester is involved?* she wondered, pushing the door open.

Patricia's question was quickly answered when a hand appeared out of nowhere, grabbed her shoulder, snatched the gun she was holding away, and yanked her out into the front room. "Move and die," a man hissed at Patricia, shoving a gun into her side. "You two…Toby…Karan…step out of there or this woman dies!"

Toby eased his head out the door, studied the situation, and knew that one wrong move would result in the death of an innocent woman." Do as Edmund orders," he told Karan and stepped through the hidden door. Karan followed.

"Throw down your gun!"

Toby reluctantly threw his gun down onto the floor and then looked up at a monster that resembled a decayed John Wayne. "Your hired killers are dead. This game is over."

"Oh no." Edmund Hayster grinned at Toby. "This game is just beginning."

chapter eight

Chief Winchester's voice was harsh and cruel. "Get downstairs!"

Patricia looked up and saw Ben, Susie, and Foster walking down the stairs. Chief Winchester was walking behind them holding a gun.

"Melinda?" Edmund asked.

"She's dead," Chief Winchester snarled. "You three…go sit on that couch. Now!"

"Do as he says," Patricia told everyone. Edmund Hayster had murder in his eyes.

Chief Winchester shook snow off a large coat and then snatched a muffler hat off his head. "We got here just in time it seems."

"Yes, our timing was perfect," Edmund agreed. "I had a feeling Melinda wasn't being honest me." Edmund motioned his gun at Patricia. "Looks like you did me a favor."

"I killed in self-defense," Patricia told Edmund, keeping her voice calm.

"Sure you did…right, Chief?" Edmund scowled.

Chief Winchester eyed Patricia. "You're going to prison for three murders…maybe even more," he promised her.

Toby eased over to Foster. "I'm sorry…son," he said in a voice that was out of character. "I only wanted better for you. I'm sorry I treated you so rough through the years. I didn't know how to show…love. I came here to find my brother…to heal us…to find myself."

Foster looked at Toby with sad eyes. "I know," he replied as if someone were digging his grave. "Mother knew you weren't a bad guy. Why do you think I stood by you all these years? You needed someone to show you…love." Foster bowed his head. "I wasn't the perfect son. I made my mistakes."

Toby reached out and squeezed Foster's shoulder. "You did as I asked. I tried to turn you into what I am because I… was dead. For that I'm sorry," he said in a broken voice. "The mistakes you made are weak compared to the monster I tried to turn you into."

"You're not a monster," Foster insisted. "I knew why you came here. I knew the secrets."

"You did?" Toby asked, taken aback.

Foster nodded. "You told me we were coming here to search for stolen jewels. I knew about Mr. Graves. I played dumb for your sake." Foster focused his eyes on Susie. "I'm not a bad guy, Susie. I treated you the way I did because I feared we were all being watched. My fears turned out to be true. I'm already in love with a woman, otherwise I might have been interested in you."

"Stephanie?" Toby asked. Foster nodded. "Stephanie is a good woman. She reminds me of your mother."

"Enough with the sappy talk," Edmund snapped at Toby and Foster. "We're here to conduct business, Toby. You can appreciate that, can't you?"

Toby narrowed his eyes. "Yes, I can," he told Edmund in a hard tone. "But you're forgetting one important fact. No one knows where the stolen jewels are hidden."

Edmund pointed his gun at Ben. "I'm sure Mr. Graves can change that fact."

Ben shook his head. "I've searched this manor through and through…still empty-handed," he told Edmund and then sat down in a chair since the couch was full. "Whoever you are…you'll never find those jewels. You can kill all of us, but you'll walk out of this cursed manor empty-handed." Ben dropped his face. "My wife is dead…Lara is dead…this place is truly cursed."

Edmund's face twisted into a knot. "Melinda assured me that you know where the jewels are hidden," he told Ben in a voice that was close to murder.

"Melinda could make a spider believe a bit of poison was a delicious, warm meal," Ben answered. He raised his eyes and watched Edmund shake snow off a gray coat with a furious hand. "If I had located the jewels, do you think I would be sitting here?"

"Don't lie to me—"

"I'm not lying," Ben told Edmund and then motioned around the front room with his right hand. "The jewels are hidden in this manor…where? Who knows? I've searched every inch…or maybe I haven't. This manor is a very old tombstone. There could be hidden places lurking about that I'm not aware of."

"We don't have time to go on a treasure hunt," Chief Winchester snapped at Edmund. "You told me Ben Graves knew the location—"

"That's what Melinda told me!" Edmund snapped back. "She was telling the truth; she had to be."

A sad chuckle left Ben's mouth. "My wife was a great liar," he said. "It took me many years to finally be able to catch on to her lies. Why I loved that woman, I'll never know."

Chief Winchester glared at Edmund with red eyes.

"Edmund, you're dropping the ball. I have two more dead bodies to deal with. I can get rid of Gary Horne because he doesn't have any family. Lara Braceton is being handled in a lawful manner in order to save face. Melinda Graves…these people…it's impossible!"

Edmund aimed his gun at Ben. "Tell me where the jewels are!" he yelled. "You're the one that's lying, not Melinda."

"Getting scared?" Karan asked Edmund. "Good. You deserve to sweat!"

"You shut up!" Edmund hollered at Karan. "You're a dead woman!"

Patricia stepped closer to Ben. *Ben's telling the truth. He doesn't know where the jewels are hidden…but he's making Edmund think he's lying. Why? What is Ben's game?* "Mr. Hayster, you can't kill everyone in this room," she warned. "I'm a well-known travel writer. My boss knows that I'm here. I've also been in contact with my boyfriend, who is a cop. He knows all about you. If anything happens to me, he's going to spend the rest of his life tracking you down. You can count on that."

Edmund aimed his gun at Patricia. "I don't scare easily," he warned her through gritted teeth. "Your little boyfriend is nothing compared to the savage dogs I've fought with in the past, do you hear me!"

Patricia ignored Edmund. She needed to focus on Chief Winchester. "Chief Winchester, my boyfriend is a cop in Georgia. His name is Brian Johnson." Patricia told Chief Winchester the town Brian worked in and even offered a phone number. "Brian knows the truth. He's been working with me on this case since Lara Braceton was murdered. When the storm ends, he's going to send all of our findings to some very powerful people and have real cops start swarming all over Whispering Hills like ants."

Chief Winchester turned pale. "This has gotten out of

hand, Edmund. You assured me you had everything under control."

"I did…I do," Edmund fired at Chief Winchester. "This woman is trying to spook you. Just calm down—and you shut up," Edmund warned Patricia.

Patricia shrugged. "Have it your way, but Chief Winchester, you already called my boss. You know I'm a travel writer. You know I don't have any reason to lie."

"Melinda did tell us about this woman," Chief Winchester told Edmund in a voice that was losing strength. "She did warn us that this woman has been involved in numerous murder cases in the past."

"I know what Melinda claimed," Edmund hissed. He looked around the room and studied everyone's faces. He ended up locking eyes with Ben. "Your wife and I have been talking for a few months. It seems like you didn't catch on to her lies. She's been playing you for a fool…making you honestly believe she was on board with your little…business adventure. Inviting Ms. McKay here was the cherry on top of the cake…or so it seemed." Edmund kept his eyes on Ben. "Our goal was to wait until you found the jewels and then kill you. But then I found out that certain people were traveling to Ohio—namely Toby and Karan."

"You should have killed them before they arrived," Chief Winchester told Edmund in a disgusted voice. "You caused us more trouble than—"

"You shut up," Edmund snapped at Chief Winchester. "I ordered Melinda to make her husband believe she was on board with his game. She called Lara Braceton and had the girl travel here—"

"Why?" Ben demanded.

"Lara Braceton was going to be our fall girl," Edmund explained. "Melinda was going to kill Toby and Karan and blame the murders on Lara…niece or not, she didn't care.

Only Lara arrived carrying far too much information inside of her head. She became a threat. Melinda killed her, but not with my permission." Edmund focused on Patricia and then looked back at Ben. "The scheme was very simple, but when Melinda killed Lara, she made matters very complicated. No matter...I'm going to clean up this mess."

"No more killings," Chief Winchester demanded. "Edmund, I have three bodies—"

"You'll do as I say or die!" Edmund warned Chief Winchester. "You're in this mess up to your neck. If you want your share of the jewels, you'll do as I say or end up spending the rest of your life behind prison bars."

"Bad cops always end up dead or in prison," Patricia told Chief Winchester and then added in a taunting voice: "Better watch your back, Chief. This guy doesn't look trustworthy... and neither was Melinda Graves. I doubt that Gary Horne was going to accept taking a few measly dollars for his services. Seems to me that Gary Horne had plans of his own and that's why Melinda Graves killed him."

Chief Winchester walked his eyes over to Edmund. He knew he couldn't trust the man. That was a fact. All Chief Winchester needed was for the stolen jewels to be found, and then he was going to pounce on Edmund and pin all the murders on him. But what about everyone else? Everybody standing before his eyes knew the truth. How in the world was he going to win the game unless he...ran? Yes, that was the ticket. After the jewels were located, he would kill Edmund, tie up his enemies, and then vanish into the storm and escape into Canada. It was the only way.

"I can watch my own back," he told Patricia. "Edmund, it's late. We need to find those jewels."

Edmund aimed his gun at Ben again. "I'm going to start killing everyone in this room, one by one, right in front of your eyes, if you don't talk."

"So, kill them," Ben said in a cold voice. "What are these

people to me? I don't know them, so don't stand there and pretend that I care." Ben raised his eyes up at Edmund. "I don't know where the jewels are, but even if I did, I wouldn't tell you. I told Ms. McKay when she arrived, I planned on getting the last laugh. And I intend to do just that."

Edmund's face began to boil. "I guess I'll have to make you talk," he threatened Ben. "Maybe a little torture might do the trick?"

What to do? Edmund Hayster and Chief Winchester both have guns. My gun is lying on the floor. If I try and go for it, I'll be shot down. My, this game of Clue certainly isn't very fun. Patricia glanced at Edmund and then at Chief Winchester. Both men were stationed in strong locations, standing a good distance apart from one another, sandwiching in everyone with deadly hands. *Have to really use my thinking skills.* "Chief Winchester, Ben has a weak heart. If Mr. Hayster tortures him his heart might give out…and then…no jewels. Just saying."

Chief Winchester looked at Ben. "Melinda didn't mention—"

"My heart medicine is in my room," Ben told Chief Winchester, following Patricia's lead. "Go check for yourself."

Chief Winchester shook his head. "Better leave this man alone, Edmund. We can't risk him dying on us…not yet."

Edmund felt as if he were being shoved into a corner. How in the world was he going to locate the stolen jewels? Ben was the ticket…but what maneuvers could Edmund utilize to make the man talk? Torture was now out of the question and the threat of killing all the guests didn't seem to bother the man.

"There's only one option," he told Chief Winchester. "We have to kill everyone, hide the bodies, and then search the manor ourselves—no matter how long it takes. After all, you are the law in this town. You can keep the outside world away from here."

"No more killings—"

"Do you really expect me to allow these people to live?" Edmund hollered at Chief Winchester. "Are you that stupid?" Edmund aimed his gun at Patricia. "Tell your boyfriend to put on his gloves, lady, because you're a dead woman."

Patricia looked at Edmund's firing finger. The monster was actually preparing to shoot her. For a brief second, she saw her life flash before her eyes...and then a warm hand touched her shoulder and calmed her heart.

"Chief!" a voice yelled.

"What...Gary?" Chief Winchester exclaimed in a startled voice. He turned to face the hidden door. Edmund released his firing finger and swung around, expecting to see Gary Horne appear. As soon as they turned away from Patricia, the lights went off.

"Down," Ben whispered, grabbing Patricia's hand.

Patricia hit the floor as bullets began flying through the air. "I was wondering when you were going to use your talent as a ventriloquist," she whispered. "You sounded just like Gary Horne."

"I tried," Ben whispered back, holding Patricia's head down against the floor as Edmund and Chief Winchester continued to fill the front room with bullets. When the firing stopped, he grabbed Patricia's hand and started crawling toward the staircase. "Follow me."

Patricia had no idea if Toby, Foster, Susie, and Karan were hurt or even alive. She heard no movement in the darkness that had enveloped the front room like a black funeral sheet. The sound of Edmund and Chief Winchester reloading their guns was the only noise that littered the air. "They're reloading...."

"Come on!" Ben shot to his legs and ran Patricia up the staircase.

Edmund opened fire, shooting into the darkness. A few bullets struck the staircase, nearly hitting Patricia and Ben. "I'm reloading...kill the others!" he roared.

The sound of the front door opening caught Chief Winchester's attention. "They're trying to get outside!" Chief Winchester ran toward the front door and tried to open fire at three shadowy figures that were escaping before his very eyes. "Stop…freeze!" he yelled, squeezing the trigger attached to his gun…only…the gun didn't fire. It was as if someone had placed their finger behind the trigger, preventing Chief Winchester from firing.

"Kill them!" Edmund yelled, struggling to reload his gun.

"My gun won't fire!" Chief Winchester continued to pull the trigger but it failed to shoot. And then he felt a cold, icy hand reach out from the darkness and touch his heart. A deep, horrifying fear entered the man's body.

"I'm getting out of here. This place is cursed!" Chief Winchester yelled in a horrible, panicked voice. He threw down his gun and burst out into the snowstorm, leaving Edmund all alone in the darkness.

Edmund crept upstairs holding a penlight in his left hand. The front door was now locked and the downstairs was secured. No one, and he meant no one, was going to take ownership of the stolen jewels except him.

"The storm will slow Toby and the others down. Maybe that coward of a cop will run into them. I have to work fast." Edmund reached the top of the stairs and began crawling down a long, dark, spooky hallway. "You can't escape!" he yelled. "I've barricaded the hidden door and broken the latch. There is no way down to the bottom floor…cooperate and I'll let you live!"

Is this guy kidding us? Patricia thought, safely standing just inside Karan's door. *Whoever this Edmund Hayster character really is, he lacks some real brains.* "Ben—" Patricia reached out her hand but felt only empty space. "Ben," she whispered, "where are you?"

"Over here," Ben whispered back, "sitting on the couch."

Something in Ben's voice put a knife in Patricia's heart. "Ben, what is it?"

"I know why my mother wanted me to burn this manor down," he told Patricia. "Even if I found the stolen jewels now, I couldn't keep them. Veronica Drakes…Henry Graves…Lara Braceton…Gary Horne…my wife—and we don't even know if Toby, Susie, and Foster are alive. The stolen jewels are covered with murder…cursed."

Patricia remained at the door. "You're right," she whispered, feeling the thick darkness shrouding the room reaching out for her with angry hands. Something was lurking in the darkness…a curse…a cruel, horrible, hungry curse. "Ben, we have to disable Edmund Hayster and Chief Winchester—"

"I know." Ben stood up and joined Patricia at the door. As he did Edmund yelled out an empty promise. "He's getting closer."

Patricia tightened her grip on an iron candle holder that was firmly planted in her right hand. "We could try to escape…."

"I tried the tunnel. Edmund broke the latch," Ben whispered. "The door won't open. Guess Melinda showed that monster all the hiding places and how to access them."

Patricia didn't like feeling trapped, but for the time being that's what she was. "I guess we have no choice but to defend ourselves."

"I guess so." Ben lifted a pocket knife that he had stored in his pants pocket. "This knife is useless against a gun, but it's all I got."

"I'm going to start checking the rooms!" Edmund threatened. "Chief Winchester is at the bottom of the stairs…

there's no way out! The rest of your friends are dead!" Edmund hoped his threats and lies would scare Patricia and Ben out of hiding. "Cooperate…make it easy on yourselves!"

"This guy is a real clown, but he sure was going to shoot me dead," Patricia whispered. She turned and looked at Ben through the darkness. "You saved my life. I just wish I knew how you made the lights go off."

"I didn't make the lights go off," Ben whispered in a solemn voice. Patricia kept her eyes on Ben but didn't say a word.

"Make it easy on yourselves and—" Edmund suddenly stopped talking, kicked open Toby's door, fired three bullets into the room, and then charged forward and began a quick search. The room, to his dismay, was empty. He returned to the hallway and aimed the penlight directly at the room door belonging to Karan.

Patricia heard Edmund begin approaching the door. "Stolen laptop," she heard her voice speak in a strange tone, as if someone had suddenly pulled the words from her mouth.

"What?"

"Someone stole Karan's laptop." Patricia felt a horrible chill run down her spine. "Ben, there's someone else in this manor." Patricia spun away from the door and looked into the darkness. "Are you in here? Please, if you are—"

"I'm here," a man's voice spoke.

"Help us," Patricia whispered.

"I intend to," the man promised, speaking in a soothing voice. "Stand away from the door."

"What is this?" Ben asked.

Patricia grabbed Ben's hand and pulled him away from the door. "Stand back and get down," she whispered, pulling Ben down behind the bed.

"Who is—"

"Down," Patricia begged.

Ben ducked down just as Edmund kicked open the door and opened fire. As soon as the bullets stopped a shadow flashed out from the darkness like a flash of lightning. All Patricia saw was a hard fist appear in the beam of light leaving Edmund's penlight. The fist struck Edmund with enough power to shake the entire manor; at least that's what it felt like to Patricia. Edmund dropped his gun and hit the floor.

"Get out of this manor and never return. Chief Winchester has fled. You are safe now," the man spoke to Patricia and Ben in a soothing but stern tone. "Tell your friend she can find her laptop in her SUV. I erased all of the data."

"Who are you?" Ben demanded.

"A friend."

"Come on, Ben," Patricia whispered. She grabbed Ben's hand and hurried him out of the room and down the stairs.

"But who—"

"I don't know," Patricia confessed, reaching the closed front door. She fought with the lock and managed to yank the front door open just as a bright flame erupted behind her.

"The front room…the front room is on fire!" Ben yelled.

"Good," Patricia yelled back and dragged Ben out into the vicious snowstorm. As she did a shadowy figure stepped forward. "Mr. Ells?" Patricia yelled over the howling winds, shielding her eyes from the snow and wind.

"Hurry!" Toby yelled. He grabbed Patricia's hand and hurried her away from the manor. Ben followed, working his way through deep snow that felt impossible to move through. Toby dragged Patricia to the front gate of the manor and stopped. To Patricia's relief Foster, Susie, and Karan were waiting at the gate unharmed—along with Chief Winchester. Chief Winchester now had his hands handcuffed behind his back. Toby had captured the fleeing criminal.

Patricia let go of Toby's hand and spun around to face the

manor. Flames were now breaking through the downstairs window. "My goodness…I certainly didn't expect the story to end this way," she stated in a shaky voice.

"But who was the man who saved us?" Ben begged Patricia as hard snow struck his thin face.

"Someone saved your life?" Toby asked. "I was just about to go inside the manor when you came out. Is someone else—"

"The man who saved our life is safe," Patricia assured Toby. "Whoever he is, he ended the curse."

"But who was he?" Ben begged.

"I guess we'll never know," Patricia told Ben and then simply grew silent and watched the flames eating the downstairs of the manor reach the second floor. "The curse is dying before our eyes, Ben," she whispered. She took Ben's hand and then sighed. "Remind me to never play the game of Clue ever again."

Ben stared at the burning manor and bowed his head. "Toby," he spoke, "I don't have a home now—"

Toby, to Patricia's relief, reached out and put his arm around Ben. "We'll start over, together, brother," he said and then reached out for his son.

Foster stepped close to Toby. "Yes, we will—Uncle."

Karan gently put her arm around Susie. "Are you okay?"

"A little shook up…but I'm okay," Susie assured her. "Maybe this was a wake-up call for me." Susie looked at the burning manor with frightened eyes. "Maybe I need to get my life together, huh?"

"Maybe we all do." Karan gently squeezed Susie's shoulder. "You'll have a friend to help you."

Well, I'll be a monkey's uncle or rear end…or whatever. All the murder suspects are turning out to be pretty decent people, Patricia thought as bright flames danced in her eyes. *So, a real treasure did emerge from that ugly, cursed manor after all…family and friendship.*

As Patricia watched the manor burn, a man dressed in a black suit escaped out of the back door, dragging a large wooden box full of stolen jewels.

"Don't worry, Dad," he said, aiming his words at Ben, "Mom kept me a secret from you, but someday I'll be back and we'll be a family...when the time is right."

Patricia didn't hear the man throw his words into the snowstorm. She was simply watching a very dangerous curse burn down to the ground. *Being a travel writer is never boring... no sir, being a travel writer is never boring indeed.*

A week later Patricia finally arrived home. Brian's car was parked in the driveway, and he was perched in front of her farmhouse. "Welcome home," he said, waved and standing in a cold rain.

Patricia, who was now driving a rental SUV because her own SUV had been burned up when the manor burned down, eased out of the driver's seat feeling like lumpy mashed potatoes. She reached for a blue umbrella, popped it open, covered her dark green winter dress, and walked over to Brian.

"Hello." She smiled and offered a very exhausted hug.

"You look horrible," Brian told Patricia and hurried her inside a warm and welcoming farmhouse.

"Home sweet home," Patricia sighed, following Brian into a kitchen that was filled with beauty and life. "Make us come coffee," she begged.

Brian watched Patricia put away her umbrella and then crash down onto a kitchen chair. "Edna give you a hard time?" he asked, sitting his own umbrella down next to the back door.

"Oh...no, Edna was actually happy with the article I turned in," Patricia explained in a tired voice. "I'm just exhausted from the drive. Susie rode with me the entire way. By the time I dropped her off at the Atlanta airport, I felt like my ears were going to fall off. That girl can talk."

Brian grinned. "The perfect ending to a very strange case, huh?" he asked.

"Kinda," Patricia sighed and then watched Brian, who was dressed like a cowboy for some reason, hurry to make a fresh pot of hot coffee. "I still can't figure out who the mystery man was. It wasn't until the very last moment that I realized someone else was hiding in that awful manor." Patricia shook her head. "Brian…I felt…an angel protecting me."

"The mystery man?"

"Oh no. He was flesh and blood," Patricia confirmed. She leaned back in the kitchen chair and studied her warm kitchen. "I thought about it and I feel…like I was meant to go to Ohio."

"I'd prefer if you stay home from now on," Brian stated, dipping fresh coffee out of a sunflower coffee can.

"Me too," Patricia agreed and began rubbing her shoulders. "I'm too pooped to pop, but you know…it was worth it. Susie has decided to go live with her parents and get her life together. Karan met an FBI agent that took a liking to her. She's going to stay up north and try to start a new life. Toby and Foster were last seen driving away with Ben, heading north toward Maine, I think—or maybe it was New Hampshire? I can't remember. I was exhausted and seeing double when I said goodbye to Ben."

"Seems like some good came out of your trip." Brian worked to put water in the old coffeepot and then sat down at the kitchen table. "I'm glad you're home, Patricia. I know you're tired, but I was hoping we could have supper at the diner tonight?"

"Oh, honey," Patricia begged, "how about we eat in? I'll

make us some soup and sandwiches and we can cuddle in front of the fireplace."

Brian smiled. "Deal. I like the idea—" Before Brian could finish his sentence Patricia's cell phone rang.

"Oh…one minute; it's probably Edna," Patricia complained. She grabbed her cell phone out of the pocket of the green dress. "No…not Edna. I don't recognize the caller."

"Maybe it's spam?"

Patricia shrugged. "I better answer it," she said and hit the green Accept button. "Hello?"

"Patricia McKay?" a voice asked.

"Yes. Who is calling, please?" Patricia asked.

"My name is Jason Millins. I'm an attorney."

"Oh…well, hello, Mr. Millins," Patricia said in a way to catch Brian's attention. Brian leaned close to her. "What can I do for you?"

"I need to confirm some information from you," Mr. Millins explained.

"Why?"

"My client is releasing a check to you. I'm in charge of the check," Mr. Millins explained.

"A check?" Patricia looked at Brian with confused eyes. "Who is your client?"

"I'm sorry, the names of all my clients are confidential," Mr. Millins informed Patricia. "All I can say is that my client asked me to pass along a message to you."

"What message?" Patricia asked. Brian shrugged as she looked at him.

Mr. Millins picked up a crisp piece of paper. "The message is this," he stated. "Dear Ms. McKay, thank you for showing such great courage in the face of danger. You renewed my hope in mankind. Please accept my gratitude. Oh, by the way, I may have saved your life in the end, but you saved my life in more ways than you will ever realize."

"The mystery man…." Patricia eyes grew wide. "I—"

"All information regarding my clients must remain confidential," Mr. Millins reminded her. He set down the paper and picked up a fancy pen. "Now, shall we get down to business, Ms. McKay?"

Patricia looked at Brian, who just shrugged his shoulders again. "Seems like you are being rewarded for a job well done."

"But I didn't save the day...." Patricia felt a tired smile touch her heart. "Maybe I did?" she said and then focused on talking with Mr. Millins. After the conservation ended, she stood up and prepared two cups of coffee. "Brian, I'm never going to figure out this world...or people. I honestly thought Toby Ells was the killer at first, but as the game continued, my list narrowed, and in the end the real killers appeared in a way I didn't expect."

Brian took his coffee from Patricia with kind, loving hands. "The world is a confusing place," he agreed. "We'll never have it figured out."

Patricia sat back down at the kitchen table and listened to a cold, hard winter rain fall. "This is one case that will be on my mind for a while. But...I'm home and after we finish our coffee, we'll need to go feed Betsy."

"Already did." Brian smiled and then added, "That cow doesn't like me."

Patricia laughed. Her laughter felt good and clean. "Did Betsy try to kick you again?" Brian nodded, grimacing. "She can be cranky and—" Patricia's cell phone rang again. This time the caller was Edna. "Oh no...not Edna."

"Throw your phone outside," Brian begged.

Patricia sighed. "I wish I could, but Edna signs my paychecks." With those words Patricia answered the call and prepared for a new adventure. Brian didn't mind. He knew the love of his life was meant to be a travel writer and explore the world. In time—when the right moment arrived—Brian knew Patricia would retire and cuddle up in his arms forever.

But for the moment Patricia McKay, the world-famous travel writer, had more mysteries to solve.

"Okay…yeah, Edna, just give me time to catch my breath for crying out loud, I just got home…. Yeah, I know you sign my paychecks…I should sock you in the nose," Patricia began to fuss. Brian just smiled.

more from wendy

Alaska Cozy Mystery Series

Maple Hills Cozy Series

Sweeetfern Harbor Cozy Series

Sweet Peach Cozy Series

Sweet Shop Cozy Series

Twin Berry Bakery Series

about wendy meadows

Wendy Meadows is a USA Today bestselling author whose stories showcase women sleuths. To date, she has published dozens of books, which include her popular Sweetfern Harbor series, Sweet Peach Bakery series, and Alaska Cozy series, to name a few. She lives in the "Granite State" with her husband, two sons, two mini pigs and a lovable Labradoodle.

Join Wendy's newsletter to stay up-to-date with new releases. As a subscriber, you'll also get BLACKVINE MANOR, the complete series, for FREE!

Join Wendy's Newsletter Here
wendymeadows.com/cozy